LIGHTHOUSE LOYALTY

LIGHTHOUSE LOYALTY

SARAH KAY BIERLE

Gazette665

To my grandmothers:

Grandma Barbara
whose enthusiastic creativity
inspired so many.
I miss you and cherish the fun memories.

Grandma Katherine
who loves the beach.
When I spend a day at the seaside with you,
I'm too happy to write.

Foreword

Sometimes we search for something and never seem to find it. Sometimes we have to create what we want. That describes my search for a family-friendly historical novel about life at a lighthouse in the 19th Century. In 2015, my wife Nancy and I met Sarah at a living history event, and it had been several years since we had seen her at Cabrillo National Monument. As we caught up on family news and historical happenings, she mentioned that her first novel was set to release. I mentioned my quest for a lighthouse novel highlighting the courage of the keepers and their families. And the rest – to be cliché – is history.

Sarah and I spent time talking about lighthouse history, touring the structure at the park, and hammering through some story details. I advised Sarah to create a fictional lighthouse location, providing direction and statistics for structures and historical details as she created "Herdman Point Lighthouse."

Taking her notes and ideas, Sarah disappeared for a while. Then the manuscripts started landing on my desk.

The story you now hold is fictional, but it firmly echoes the history of lighthouse keeping and reflects the courage, loyalty, and struggles. The men and women who tended the lighthouses brought a sense of dedication and responsibility to what was truly a 24/7 job with no days off and no sick leave. In this day of intense automation, they remain a worthy role model for the 21st Century. Though not the original story I might have imagined, *Lighthouse Loyalty* skillfully delves into questions and realities about family life and secrets. The conflict is strengthened by the lighthouse setting.

With great pleasure, I add this forward to Sarah's book. It's not often that my wife and I meet a young person with a passion for history, education, and writing. To watch Sarah take on this project at our suggestion has been a journey. You hold the journey's destination in your hands.

May this story inspire you to evaluate the lives of American lightkeepers and their families, drawing the best character qualities from their lives and incorporating them into your own life. As Keeper Arnold says in the story, "Come, let us shine a brilliant light."

Robert Munson
Historian

El Cajon, California
August 2017

INTRODUCTION

It has been many, many years since I saw Herdman Point Lighthouse, yet the first months my family spent there shaped my future, laying the foundations for a happy, contented, and loyal character. I am now in that season of life when my grandchildren sit by my chair and say, "Tell us about the lighthouse."

I answer their request, "Don't you want to ask your grandfather about the Spanish American War?" already knowing what their answer will be. They shrug and tell me, "Later. Tell us about your cat, and your uncle, and your war." And so I tell them. Again and again. The lighthouse story seems simple, and it never fails to entertain them. Perhaps – through the story – I will be able to share and teach the same character qualities my parents instilled in me.

Last summer we were all at the seaside, and as we watched our children and grandchildren rambling in the shadow of a nearby lighthouse, my husband said simply, "Write your story, Susan." And when the next winter came, I did.

Seated by the cozy fire while the New England snows banked outside the house, I tried to walk in those little girl shoes again – to only tell the story as it unfolded in my nine-year-old world. To remember all the lessons about loyalty. To relive in memory everything that happened in those first months at that new lighthouse. Sometimes, perhaps, words or descriptions have slipped into the manuscript that would have been beyond that little girl's understanding, but I know the circumstances. I lived and experienced it all. The details are what I saw and knew at that time, even if the language of the story is sometimes more mature. Through the writing process, I have tried not to judge those girlish thoughts and conclusions too harshly, but to simply tell what happened.

Truly, this is the way it was. I remember the details, the emotions – all of it so vividly. It's almost as if I was there again in 1867.

Chapter 1

"This is my new home," I thought, leaning against the railing of the ship and gazing toward the lighthouse. Graceful and solid, the stone lighthouse stood securely on the rocks, its tower and lantern rising a little above the roof of the house to send a warning beacon to the passing ships. The small ship that had brought me and my family to our new post anchored safely in the little cove, away from the rocks on my left where the waves tossed and foamed around the half-submerged boulder peaks, jutting out from the coast into the Long Island Sound. The early afternoon sun broke through the dull winter clouds, casting a cheery light on the gray-toned land and the deep blue water.

Hunching my shoulders, I shivered and tried to make sense of my feelings. A tinge of excitement that Father had been assigned to this important post dampened by regret over leaving our lighthouse on Lake Erie with its nearby town and

friendly families. I had said good-bye to my best friends, Jane
and Anna, and I wasn't sure I would like the remoteness of
the new lighthouse. How would I fill the days between winter
storms or the long summer afternoons without attending
school, running through the grassy field, or wading in the
shallows with my friends?

Tears pricked my eyes, and I couldn't help noticing the
differences when compared to my former lighthouse home
along the Great Lake. There, the water had lapped quietly at
the shore, and our light had been a warning for the nearby
shoal. The lake water could get fierce and nasty in a storm,
but there was not the water's murmur and crash that I heard
now. My father had been a lighthouse keeper as long as I could
remember. I was born at a lighthouse, and for the entire nine
years of my life, I'd lived in lighthouses. I always thought I'd
love that life, but as I watched the water beating endlessly on
the rocks, I wished for the hundredth time we hadn't moved.

Heavy footsteps approached, and Uncle Richard – Mama's
brother and Father's assistant lightkeeper – joined me at the
railing. I frowned to myself, careful to look away so he wouldn't
see the expression. Leaving my friends and living along a stretch
of lonely coastline was challenging enough. Having a stranger
join our family – even if he was a relative – didn't make the
change easier. I'd never met him until yesterday, but Mama
had told me and my younger brothers about him.

I glanced up at my uncle. He was tall, but other than his
height and strength, he didn't match the character in Mama's
stories. Ever since we met him yesterday on the dock, he hadn't

laughed or told a joke, and he now stood silent, holding his long coat tightly around him in a protective way. When my brothers had asked him to tell a story, he'd gruffly said he didn't know any worth telling.

"It's a quiet, lonely place, isn't it?" Uncle Richard murmured. I wasn't sure if he was talking to me or himself, but I replied, "Yes."

I pushed back a strand of my hair, flapping in front of my eyes, then rubbed my gloved hands and tried to warm my chilly fingers. Shivering in the late winter wind, I tried to cheer up, thinking of Father's pride when he had been specially asked to take this post because of his care and watchfulness. Leaving Lake Erie behind, we had travelled by train to a port town where we had boarded this small ship to complete the journey to the lighthouse. Quite an adventure for 1867! My younger brothers – Jacob and Paul – had thought the shrill whistle, rattle of the rail cars, and bustling crowd at the stations was all part of a grand adventure.

"Do you like trains? Have you ridden on one?" I asked Uncle Richard, feeling awkward in the silence. It wouldn't hurt to get better acquainted since he was my uncle and would be stuck with us for who knew how long.

"Do you?" he answered, avoiding my question.

"It was exciting. But so noisy and so many people. That is – it would've been exciting if I hadn't been leaving my friends. Jane will be top of the spelling class now that I'm gone. We always competed for first. And Anna's brother will have finished her dollhouse by now. He was a soldier in the war, and he can't walk anymore, but he makes the most wonderful toys. And if it's not snowing too much, they're all going to the church choir concert this Sunday evening." I had to stop or else I'd start crying. After waiting and not thinking about everything I'd miss, I said in a steady voice, "If you could live here, in a big city, or a little village, what would you choose?"

"I prefer quiet," Uncle Richard said pointedly. I blushed, suddenly realizing my uncle wasn't interested in my chattering.

"Susan," Mama called, from where she sat on one of our large trunks, holding my baby sister, "could you please go find your brothers? Your father should be coming back soon to take us ashore."

"Yes, Mama," I responded, going to her and thankful to slip away from my uncle. "Are you feeling alright?" Mama always got dreadful headaches and didn't feel well when she had to travel on a boat. She had been disappointed that we didn't go overland from the city to our lighthouse, but the inspector insisted by water was the quickest way and had left orders for us to meet him at the lighthouse.

Mama's eyes looked tired, but she smiled, reaching up to straighten the ribbons on her purple bonnet. "I'm alright, daughter, but will be most thankful when we're ashore. At least Marian has been good." She pulled the sleeping baby's blanket a little tighter.

I heard giggles from somewhere on the deck and hurried off to find my brothers. They were by the goat's pen, poking bits of hay toward the friendly animal and jumping excitedly when she took the offered food. "Look, Susan, look," shouted six-year-old Jacob, his brown eyes full of mischievous fun and his smile revealing the gap of his missing front teeth. "Patches likes us."

"Yes, she likes us," five-year-old Paul echoed. "Come, see." He reached out, took my hand, and pulled me over to the pen. Patches tried to nibble Paul's hair, then pushed at my hand, looking for food. I took off my glove and ran my hand over her smooth white coat, splotched with random brown markings, like someone had sewn patches on her. In their nearby cage, five plump hens clucked and fluffed.

"What color do you think Patches's baby will be?" Paul asked. "Brown or white?" Ever since Father had said Patches would have a kid in the spring, my youngest brother had been concerned about this.

"I don't know, but Mama wants us to come," I replied. "Father will be back soon."

"Alright, Susan," Jacob answered. He reached up and combed his dark hair to one side, then dashed forward on the boat.

"Can I just feed Patches one more handful?" Paul pleaded, his eyes full of sympathy for the supposedly hungry goat. I agreed, and then we went and sat on the trunks which the crew had moved to the deck in preparation for going ashore.

Jacob and Paul kicked their heels against the trunks, and I tapped my foot in a fidgety way until a weary glance and tight smile from Mama made us stop. I slid from trunk to trunk to sit beside Mama and whispered, "Is Uncle Richard unhappy about being an assistant lightkeeper?" We both looked at him, standing at the far railing, expressionless and alone.

"I think it's different than what he thought he would do. Or wanted to do."

"He doesn't seem friendly."

"Give him a little time. He went through some struggles last year, and he doesn't know you and the boys well. If you and your brothers are respectful and friendly to him, I have no doubt you'll get along fine in a week."

"You mean he could be a friend?" I asked doubtfully. "He would want to have tea with me and my doll?"

Mama smiled. "Not a friend the way Jane and Anna were. But you may find some common interests. Uncle Richard loved to read and probably still does."

"I like to read...as long as it's not a geography lesson." I looked toward my uncle. Maybe Mama was right. Hopefully, in a few days we would be friends, and he would be happy living with our family. I smiled for the first time that morning. After all, Anna and Jane hadn't liked reading big books and hadn't wanted to discuss stories.

On shore, I spotted Father walking down the path. Finally! I couldn't wait to get off the ship, but then I remembered we had to meet the inspector – an official who came to the lighthouse two or three times each year to inspect the record books, bring supplies and mail, and decide if we were following the rules and regulations created by the Lighthouse Board for lightkeeping. At that remembrance, I wished Father would slow down, but too soon the rowboat bumped against the ship, and he climbed the rope ladder, poking his head up to see us.

"Ready to go ashore?" Father called. "The boat's here so you don't have to swim," he finished with a comical expression. "I spoke with Inspector Milton and Mr. and Mrs. Vendal. Everything is in order for us to take over lightkeeping here at Herdman Point. Ho!" he exclaimed, snatching his cap as the wind threatened to carry it off and clamping it back on his short, curly hair.

Father's cheerfulness momentarily reassured me. Maybe the inspector was especially nice. Jacob, Paul, and I ran to the side of the ship and looked down at Father, waiting for instructions to get into the small row boat. His blue eyes twinkling with amusement at his jokes, he pointed at us playfully, counting. "Excellent. I have all my children here. Now, where's Richard?"

I pointed to Uncle Richard, who had moved to the bow of the ship and stood looking out at the sea. Father shook his head slightly when he saw his brother-in-law but didn't say whatever he thought. "Richard, we're goin' ashore," Father called. "Inspector Milton wants to see all of us – including my new assistant. The crew has agreed to bring ashore our trunks in the second boat."

I held Marian while Mama climbed into the boat, then handed my baby sister to Father and waited for the boys to scramble down. When it was my turn to descend, I gripped the railing of the sturdy ship, afraid to step on the ropes, worried that the wind would catch my skirts and I would fall into the blue-green water. I heard Father's voice telling me to come, face the ship, hold tight, and step down. Holding on to the wobbly ropes for dear life, I placed each foot after the other – careful not to catch the short heel of my boots. At the last moment, my right foot slipped, but Father caught me and set me down in the rocking dory. Uncle Richard sprang in last, pitching the boat. Mama groaned, and the boys laughed.

Father and Uncle Richard rowed with quick, steady strokes toward the shore. I sat beside Mama in the stern of the boat, facing the men. Father's expression – even as he rowed – was cheery and determined. There were only two things that really upset my father: laziness and dishonesty. As he often reminded us children, hard work and truthfulness were necessary for an upright life and absolutely essential for a lighthouse keeper and family. Uncle Richard's expression was harder to understand, but I hadn't known him more than a few hours. He seemed preoccupied with something and occasionally glanced around him, as if expecting an unpleasant surprise.

"Is Inspector Milton nice?" I softly asked Father.

"He is a fair man, I think," Father replied. "We won't have any trouble since we follow the rules."

But what if Uncle Richard doesn't follow the rules? I thought. Though Father always obeyed the rules exactly and was praised for his work, the inspectors still frightened me. Lighthouses were government property; we lived in them, but anyone – inspector, citizen, or military – could come to the house, expecting to find hospitality and order. If the inspector thought the lighthouse wasn't clean or we were wasting supplies, he could dismiss us in disgrace.

The boat scraped alongside the rickety dock and mooring place, and I tried not to remember how far we were from friends or a town. Mama glided up the inclined path beside Father, carrying Marian and seeming perfectly pleased at the idea of living here. The boys and I marched after them, and Uncle Richard lagged behind.

"Do you like it here?" I asked Mama as we stood together in the yard after the men had gone inside to finish business.

"I'll learn to like it," she replied.

"Don't you think it's a little far from a town or civil... civilize..." I struggled with the big word.

"Civilization," Mama said. "It is. But there wasn't a large town near our old home when we first moved there. When I left my family and work as a fashionable seamstress in New Bedford years ago, I made up my mind to try to be content and cheerful wherever we lived." Mama studied my face for a moment, and I was certain she knew that I missed my friends and didn't like it here.

I resented that, but before I could assure her that I was... (I didn't know what I would say without lying), a middle-aged lady in a pretty dress and travelling bonnet came out the front door and greeted Mama pleasantly. "Mrs. Arnold, I presume? I'm Mrs. Vendal," she spoke in a rapid, breathless way. "Welcome to Herdman Point. I have done my best to make sure the house was as clean as I could make it, and I hope you and your family will be happy here."

"Thank you," Mama replied, shaking hands with Mrs. Vendal.

Mrs. Vendal looked back at the lighthouse and wiped her eyes with her handkerchief. "I am sorry to be leaving the place." She hesitated, then went on quickly. "But my husband is not well, and I cannot keep up the work all on my own. The last months have been hard. Our assistant keeper – Mr. Dunbar – well, he was not a good man. Took to drinking and seemed troubled by memories of the war. Nothing we said made any difference. He was removed by the inspector."

Mama nodded sympathetically, and I stood at her elbow, looking at the lighthouse and letting the conversation swirl around me. Mrs. Vendal talked and talked, seeming to be glad for conversation with another lady. "Then, poor Mr. Vendal took a turn for the worse. He had got a bad wound in the last days of the war – during the Appomattox Campaign in '65, nearly two years ago – and it never healed properly. He goes through painful times when he can't get out of bed…"

The war. It was over, but the older I got the more I noticed its effects – Anna's crippled brother, the black mourning dresses worn by Mrs. Daves, Mrs. Henderson, and Mrs. Schulz. We just didn't talk about the fighting much in my family, and I wondered about it. I'd have to remember to ask Father about it sometime.

"Oh, but we did love it here," Mrs. Vendal was saying when I refocused on her bobbing bonnet and her hands twisting her gloves. "And, except for Mr. Dunbar's bad manners, were very happy. I am sorry to leave, but," she gave a trembling smile, "I am sure you will take good care of the place."

Mama assured her we would do our very best, asked about the weather at Herdman Point, and inquired about the lighthouse. My mama had a gift for comforting people by listening and talking with them. She seemed absolutely perfect to me. Her responses, her expressions – everything was ladylike and genuine. It was such a conflict for me; I wanted to be exactly like her when I grew up, but today convinced me that I was selfish.

At a break in the ladies' conversation, Mrs. Vendal turned toward me, saying, "Miss Susan? I believe your mother told me that was your name." I nodded politely, and she continued. "There's a cat here. Her name is Mattie. Unfortunately, Mr. Dunbar was very cruel and used to kick her and pull her tail. I've been trying to make friends with Mattie and help her understand she doesn't need to be afraid. Could you watch out for her and be friendly to her?"

Outwardly copying Mama, I beamed and replied, "Yes, Mrs. Vendal. I'd be happy to. I've never had a pet before, but I've always wanted one." She smiled reassuringly.

Mr. Vendal limped from the doorway to his wife's side and leaned on his cane. "My dear, it is time to go. They've taken our trunks down to the boat."

Mrs. Vendal nodded and dabbed her eyes with her handkerchief. She took something from the pocket of her long skirt and pushed it into Mama's hands. "I had wanted to plant these to make the rocky yard brighter," she murmured swiftly. "It is February, but spring is coming. Please take them and plant them. Good-bye. God keep you." She nodded with finality and walked down the path, matching her pace to her husband's slow stride.

"What is it?" I asked, reaching for the baby so Mama could open the packet. She folded back the brown paper, and we peered inside. Seeds for flowers and vegetables. We looked at the barren rocky yard of our new home, then down at the seeds in her hands, and smiled at each other. "It will help," I said, scuffing at the drab colored ground and trying not to compare it to the coming springtime grasses along the lake.

Father and Uncle Richard came out of the house with a short, stocky man who had a very solemn expression. "And you completed the transaction for the furniture with the Vendals, I hope?" he said as they stepped off the low front steps and came toward us.

"Yes, we paid them a fair price for their furniture, and," Father turned to Mama, "we should have a nice housekeeping." When we left our old lighthouse, Father had sold most of our possessions, except our clothes, books, good linens, and family treasures. My painted bedstead and little rocking chair had been sold because Father had explained that it was too expensive to transport our furniture and had said we would buy what we needed.

"Inspector Milton," Father said, introducing us to the gentleman, "this is my family." Mama curtsied politely, and

I followed her example, then waved Marian's little hand. A shiver ran along my spine as I greeted this judge of lightkeepers.

"Samuel Arnold, I'm sure you and your family will do well here," the inspector said courteously. "You're a good lighthouse keeper and family from what I've heard. And you," Inspector Milton squinted at Uncle Richard, "are you sure we haven't met before?"

"I don't think so, sir," Uncle Richard said, looking confused.

Inspector Milton edged closer, staring at Uncle Richard with a frown. "You weren't some Rebel raider or something during the war?"

"No, sir." Uncle Richard stood stiffly and seemed to force himself not to look away from his questioner.

"Hmm…" the doubtful inspector replied.

"Sir," Uncle Richard spoke respectfully, "I solemnly promise you to do my duty as an assistant lightkeeper. My past should not matter to you."

"Good enough…for now. We will talk again some other time," Inspector Milton replied, before turning abruptly and heading down the trail. Father looked at Uncle Richard, but my uncle shrugged and wouldn't meet Father's eye. At that moment, I wondered if something was wrong. Could my uncle have a secret? Or was he simply nervous in a new place and job?

The boys ran around the corner of the building and stood near me, panting. Father deliberately looked away from Uncle Richard to smile at Mama.

"A new home," he said, looking up at the light tower. "Where there is hard work, loyalty, and family love, there is light." He grabbed Mama's hand with playful possession. "Come, Harriet, my dear. Let's work to send forth a brilliant light."

Jacob and Paul ran ahead of them, carrying chunks of speckled rocks. "Race you to the top!" Jacob shouted.

"Ladies don't race, and we are ladies," I said, holding Marian closer and walking with exaggerated dignity.

At the door, I looked back. Uncle Richard had walked the opposite direction – away from us, toward the rocks – and was staring at the sea. As though he was still reluctant to come near the lighthouse and create its searching beams. As though he was a stranger ashore, unwilling to make friends – even with his family.

Remembering Mama's words, I whispered to Marian, "We'll befriend him. Somehow." Glancing up at the lighthouse tower, I added to myself, "I hope I'll learn to like this lighthouse."

Chapter 2

Clattering down the stairs and into the main room where Mama and I were unpacking, the boys returned with a report. "Ten rooms, Susan," Jacob called, after his third round of counting. "And that includes the storage rooms and watchroom, but not the two closets."

"And three hallways," Paul chimed in.

"No, two," Jacob retorted.

"Three."

"Two!"

"Boys, boys," Mama said, glancing with an alarmed look toward Marian who slept peacefully in a nest of blankets in an empty packing box. "That's enough. You'll wake the baby. Really it just depends on how you count the hallway upstairs. No reason to argue."

"Have you found Mattie yet?" I asked, lifting the heavy dictionary out of a box and stacking it with the other smaller books.

The boys shook their heads, but that didn't exactly surprise me. Galloping all over the house was probably not the best way to find and befriend a shy cat. I wondered who I would make friends with first – my uncle or the cat.

Above us, the sounds alternated between scraping, sliding, and thumping as Father and Uncle Richard moved bedsteads, slid chairs, and placed trunks in the bedrooms. By the time Mama had unwrapped all her pretty china dishes and put them on the shelf in the kitchen, they called that the rooms were ready for us to make the beds and unpack the trunks.

In the entryway, Uncle Richard hoisted his large sea chest, and I followed him up the stairs. He lugged the heavy box into his room in the upper back corner of the lighthouse, then closed the door. I ducked into my small, barren bedroom and opened my traveling trunk which already stood in the corner.

Three dresses, underclothes and nightgowns, my bag of hair ribbons, my doll – Mary – and a gift from Jane and Anna. The present was a new notebook and pencil; they had written their addresses on the inside cover and penciled "don't forget to write us letters." As if I could ever forget my dearest friends! I set aside the journal, hung my dresses on the pegs behind the corner curtain, positioned the little hard bench, and spread the blue and white nine patch quilt Mama had left for me over the layers of blankets on the bed. The curtains would have to be hung later because I couldn't reach that high.

Now I was settled in my room, but – as I looked out the window – I already missed the snowy landscape in winter and the lush green meadows in spring at our old home.

The view here? Just rocks and water, water and rocks. I could faintly hear Patches bleating in the stable shed where she'd been tethered and the hens stowed to keep them safe and out of the cold.

"We like it here. It's sure a lots bigger lighthouse," Jacob announced as the boys entered my room.

"Oh, go away," I said crossly. "You and your cheerfulness. Just leave me alone for a little while can't you?"

"Grumpy sis," Paul whispered loudly, hiding behind Jacob when I frowned at him.

"Say, do you like Uncle Richard?" Jacob asked. "He sure doesn't seem as wonderful as he did in Mama's stories. Do you think Mama wasn't telling the truth?"

"Mama doesn't lie. Now, go away."

Early dusk came, and I could hear Father and Uncle Richard talking as they worked on the light. It would beam brightly from the moment the sun touched the western horizon to the time when sunrise was complete the next day. Those were the rules from the Lighthouse Board, and every lightkeeper in America had to follow them. And there were unwritten rules for lighthouse daughters: help Mama.

I went downstairs, and behind the closed door to the main room, I paused with my hand on the handle. "But why's she upset?" I heard one of the boys ask.

"It's not always easy to leave home and friends," Mama's voice replied.

"But this is home."

"Yes. Let's just be patient. It will be alright in a few days."

Mama knew then. She knew I was sad about leaving my friends. I wanted to be perfect, to be just like her. And now she knew that I wasn't. That's it, I decided. I'm going to do whatever it takes. I'm not going to talk about our old home. I'm not going to talk about my friends. I'm not going to let anyone know that I'm lonely. And even if that doesn't help, at least no one will ever know I'm unhappy.

During the next several days I kept busy, helping Mama settle everything just the way she wanted it. The lighthouse began to feel like home; the books were on the shelves, Mama's favorite blue curtains crisply framed the windows, our little toys piled in a corner box, and Father had tacked his almanac near his desk in the parlor. I let myself think of it as home and found that some of the comparisons dulled. Once Mama asked me if I missed Jane and Anna, but I dashed for Marian who had started wailing and accomplished two goals at once: to help Mama and not think about my friends. Mama thought my little sister might be getting her first tooth soon because she fretfully wanted to be held most of the time. She was too little to tell tales about the tears in my eyes.

In the flurry of starting a new housekeeping routine and finding storage places for our things, Uncle Richard settled into a quiet role in the family. He kept his thoughts to himself and worked readily. But something was wrong. The boys tagged after him, asking again for stories; he didn't send them away but gruffly repeated he had no stories to tell. Mama invited him to have a cup of tea and conversation with her and Father one afternoon, but he declined and said he was tired and going to rest; that might have been normal for an assistant lightkeeper, except twenty minutes earlier Uncle Richard had announced he'd adjusted to his schedule easily and wasn't tired. Marian terrified him, and he didn't even want to learn how to hold a sweet baby. Once when I went up to the watchroom during his early evening watch to ask if he wanted any coffee, he turned quickly at the soft sound of my shoes and seemed to be ready to tackle a stranger. Who would he be afraid of, especially in this faraway place?

He was part of the family, and yet he wasn't. I asked Mama why he wasn't friendlier, and she admitted she didn't know what was wrong. Only Father seemed to understand Uncle Richard, giving him time to learn his new tasks.

One afternoon Mama asked me to smooth and fold the crumpled, outdated newspapers we had used for packing. I pressed the papers flat and folded them on the original folds. Words, words, words, covering the yellowing pages. Headlines announcing victories and defeats in the past war. I wanted to read these, to learn more about the war that I had been too little to understand when it happened. When I finished the task, I took the top paper to Mama, asking, "May I read this? I haven't had anything new to read in a while."

Mama scanned the pages quickly and handed them back. "Yes. I'm not sure you will understand it or find it very interesting, but you're welcome to read it. Remember, reading time is when your chores are done."

I turned to head to my reading corner and then realized I hadn't chosen a cozy reading place at this lighthouse. At our old lighthouse, a comfortable corner in the pantry had been my hidey-hole for daydreams and reading. I decided my new bedroom seemed too commonplace and comfortable, and the upstairs hallway was too busy with the boys running around.

I went to the front entrance and started walking through the house, looking for just the right place. The entrance hall was drafty, and the oil storage room and general storage room with its workbench were too cluttered. Peeking into the parlor, I saw Father explaining the recordkeeping books to Uncle Richard as they sat in front of the large desk beneath the ticking clock.

"Why the troubled look, daughter?" Mama asked, glancing up from her knitting as I turned from the parlor to look at the main room. "Weren't you going to read for a little while?"

"I can't find a special place to sit," I explained.

"Not this cozy room?" Mama questioned, motioning to the long table and benches, chairs, fireplace, and round braided rug.

"I love this room," I admitted. "But it's the center of everything in our home and not quiet."

"You don't need too much quiet. I don't want you to be lonesome," Mama said. "We'll be starting school lessons again soon."

"Oh, I'm fine, I think." And when I said it, I really did believe it.

I peeked into the kitchen. With the fire whispering in the stove, the delicious scents from Mama's cooking, and the stacks and stacks of dishes that I got to dry after each meal, the kitchen would be too distracting for the perfect reading place. I sighed and turned away.

Wandering upstairs, I walked through the bedroom hallway. My parents' room was across from mine, and Baby Marian slept snuggly in a cozy wooden box beside their big bed at night. Behind me, I heard Uncle Richard coming up the stairs. "Is the recordkeeping hard?" I said as he passed me in the hallway.

"Oh, no, not bad at all," he answered cheerily, pausing with his hand on the door handle of his room. "I've kept records for ships. It's not much different."

"Which ships? Where did you sail?" I asked, hoping for a long awaited story.

"I was first mate on a few merchant ships and captain twice. Stories another time, Susan." He ducked into his room so quickly that he seemed to escape. I stood there looking at the closed door, trying to imagine my uncle in charge of a ship. Shrugging, I turned the hallway corner, passed the boys' room, and climbed the stairs leading into the light tower.

Herdman Point Lighthouse didn't have a tall, tall tower reaching into the clouds, like the ones Father described on the Southern coast. Our tower was just the stairs, watchroom, and then a ladder, leading through a trapdoor to the glass enclosure called the lantern where every night the light burned and the lens reflected.

A single straight-backed chair stood in the watchroom near the glass-paned window which looked out toward the sea. There wasn't much room for anything else, but here in this tiny room, Father and Uncle Richard took turns watching through the night. Their watches were prescribed in the lighthouse rules, and they traded every four hours, ensuring that either keeper or assistant keeper was always there to watch the light. They waited through those long hours from sunset to sunrise, alert to any change in the brightness, the turning speed and light flashes, and listening for any signs of danger on the sea. The stray wood shavings scattered on the floor and the book propped open on the chair hinted at their midnight activities.

Then I noticed the ladder, leading up to the light itself. I climbed one of the wide wooden rungs, turned around, and sat down on the deep, comfortable step. I leaned back against the side, pressing my shoulder in the ladder's corner, and it gave me a comfortable hug. With a satisfied wriggle, I knew I'd found the perfect place. I flicked open the newspaper, ready to see what I could learn about the war.

A faint meow distracted me. I glanced up anxiously. Mattie? Yes, there, a calico cat poked her nose curiously into the watchroom. After my days of searching, she had appeared when she was ready. Delighted to finally see her, I cautiously stepped down and then crawled across the floor, anxious to win her friendship with a gentle pat. "Here, Mattie... Aren't you a pretty cat?" She stared at me for a second with scared eyes, turned, pressed against the wall, and darted back down the stairs. I plopped flat on the floor and leaned my head on my hand, discouraged. I was only going to be nice. Didn't Mattie know that? Why was she still afraid?

Father startled me as he came up the stairs, carrying an oil can and polishing cloth. "Susan Rose, why don't you sit in the chair?" He shook his head but smiled indulgently. "Little ladies shouldn't lie on the floor like that."

"Sorry." I moved to a kneeling position. "Did you see the cat? Mattie?"

"If that was the colorful blur that darted by me on the staircase, then yes. Was she up here with you?" Father set down his can and stepped up on the ladder to unfasten the trap door.

"Yes, but then she got scared. Mrs. Vendal told me Mattie wasn't treated very nicely, but I thought she would know I wanted to be friendly."

"It might take some time. Be patient with her. Your fault, Susan Rose, is impulsiveness." He tugged on my braid affectionately and started up the ladder. "You don't like to wait, and you'll do just about anything to get results now. This might be a good life lesson for you." He looked down at me. "Want to hand up the oil can?"

As he leaned down through the trapdoor, I stepped up a couple ladder rungs, balancing the heavy can. Father always let us children help around the lighthouse with tasks we could accomplish. He'd promised when I was older he would teach me how to keep a light burning and turning through the night.

When I settled on my ladder seat, I couldn't concentrate on the articles. I thought about Father. We didn't always see him much – he had to stay awake for the night watches, work or sleep during the day, and couldn't always eat supper with us. There were days when he was tired, and on those days, he got frustrated easily. Still, I always knew he could fix any leaky shingles, scraped knees, hurt feelings, or burned bread with hard work, care, or love. And he'd never – as far as I could remember – intentionally broken a lighthouse rule or allowed his family to.

A while later Uncle Richard marched up the stairs, humming something under his breath. "Did you have a nice rest?" I asked, climbing off the ladder.

"Couldn't sleep," he sighed.

"I think we may have a rainstorm," Father called down. "The wind is rising. And the sea has a different tone. I can't quite describe how it sounds."

Uncle Richard bent down to look out the low window. "It has lost something," he said softly, his voice catching. "It's mourning." Before I could say anything, he rose and briskly climbed the ladder.

He was right. That is what it sounded like, but I would not have thought to describe the sea that way. Why did he?

Chapter 3

The mournful whisper of the sea rang in my ears a few days later as I sat in the watchroom, following the printed newspaper lines with my finger. I'd finished every word of the first paper and thought I had a pretty good understanding that Rebels were bad men who'd been disloyal to our grand country. If they were all like those horrible bushwhackers, they ought to be hanged. That article had been simply terrifying.

1864 was the date on the paper I read today. A report about a battle at a place I couldn't even say. I tried sounding it out: S-p-o-t-s-y-l-v-a-n-i-a Court House. I wasn't sure who won; I guessed the Union men had beat the Rebels, but then the long, long columns with the names of dead and injured men made me wonder.

Jolly singing in the lantern above distracted me, and I frowned up the ladder. Father's sea songs were not the right accompaniment for war tragedies. But maybe I could ask him about the battle and the war. "Father, can I come up?" I called, looking skyward through the little trapdoor.

"Yes, Susan Rose," he replied, pausing in the tune. Leaving the newspaper on the low windowsill, I put both hands on the steep ladder and climbed higher until I was standing on the narrow walkway between the large light lens and the outer protective glass of the lantern.

The glass and walls of the lantern protected the delicate lens and flickering oil lamps from bad weather, winds, birds, and other elements. Outside the lantern, another narrow balcony encircled it. Father and Uncle Richard could stand out there to wash the lantern windows, but the strong winds could be dangerous and we children couldn't go out there alone.

Father cleaned away the dark soot on the lens with a soft cotton cloth. I had often watched him at our old lighthouse, but today was the first time I'd explored the lantern here at Herdman Point. "Is it a good lens, Father?" I asked.

"A beautiful one," he said admiringly. "Just think, Susan Rose, this lens was made far across the sea in France and brought here to help us guard the coast."

"Why don't we make the lenses here in America?" I wondered, examining the delicately cut crystal and trying to think how I wanted to ask about the war.

"The design of these lenses was developed by a Frenchman – Mr. Fresnel – and they have the proper equipment to make them over there. The lenses had been available since the early part of this century, but it wasn't until our lighthouses came under the direction of the Lighthouse Board in the 1850's that the Fresnel lens became widely used in our country."

"Why, Father?"

"Because the men in charge of the lighthouses before had not wanted to spend the extra money for the beautiful lenses," he said, sighing. "It is the delicate balance of efficiency and budgeting."

"What did they use before the Fresnel lenses?" I wondered aloud.

"Oh, all kinds of things. Mirrors, metal reflectors. And the lamps weren't as good back then, not as bright. Sometimes candles were used or poor quality oil."

I peered inside the lens where the lamps sat with coiled wicks, trimmed, filled with oil, and ready to be lit at sunset. It was light imprisoned. Imprisoned to give life. The thought made me hopefully sad, reminding me of my secret promise. No one would know when I was lonely. Imprisoning a secret to be cheerful and helpful to others, so they would think I was brave.

"There we are. Finished now," Father announced, folding up his cloth. "Susan Rose, I have to go outside on the walk and clean off the bugs on the glass. Is there anything you should be helping your mother with?"

"No, she told me I did my chores well and that I could read."

Thousands of dead men, I thought, remembering the article. Had the war really even happened? Who could believe there was such darkness in the world when a ray of sunlight broke through the cloudy sky, making the water sparkle? Father motioned for me to come outside. I clung to the metal railing with one hand and battled the cold wind from whipping my skirts. The sea rippled, and a few boats sailed close to the horizon.

"A nice winter day, isn't it?" Father called, from the other side of the lantern where he was scrubbing away a squished bug, his efforts making a squeaky sound. He came and stood by me a few moments later, then opened the small door so we could re-enter the lantern.

"Father, what was the battle? And who won it?" I asked as stood inside, looking out at the sea.

"Which battle? And are you talking about the recent war or a different one?"

"I can't say it, but I can spell it. The battle at S-p-o-t-s-y-l-v-a-n-i-a Court House. It was in 1864."

"That must've been one of Grant's battles. I think it was a Union victory. What has you so interested in the war, daughter?"

"Mama said I could read some of the newspapers. I want to understand it all now since I was too little when it happened."

"You are still a bit too young to understand it all. I'm not sure if anyone will completely understand the causes and the outcomes for a long while yet."

"Do you think the Rebels were bad men, Father?"

"There are always good and bad men on both sides, but I didn't agree with the Confederates' views on government and slavery."

"You didn't have to be a soldier."

"No. I was already working for the government as a lighthouse keeper. They needed loyal Union men at the Great Lakes lighthouses."

"Why's that?"

Father glanced down at me. "Another story for when you're a bit older. Now, my advice: don't believe everything you read in the newspapers."

I nodded. "Can I ask Uncle Richard about the war?"

"You can, but when I asked him, he wasn't interested in talking about it."

I inwardly debated whether I should ask the question that had been troubling me for a couple days. Finally, I said, "Do you like Uncle Richard, Father?"

"I don't have any reason to dislike him," he answered. "Is something wrong?"

"He's not very friendly."

"He thinks he's had bad luck. From his letters, Mama and I know he lost a ship."

"How?"

"I don't know. As long as he does his work properly, I don't want to ask too many questions right now. The sea and life as a merchant mariner is all he's known. Try to remember that even though we're all family, he has to learn to trust us. Trust is part of the sea-faring culture that he and I grew up in."

"But I thought you sailed on a whaling ship and wasn't Uncle Richard on a merchant ship?"

"Yes, but there are similar aspects. Trust has to be earned, and loyalty can't be bought."

In the afternoon, I saw Uncle Richard in the upstairs hallway, carrying a book. "What are you reading?" I asked, pointing to the plain cover.

"Shakespeare." He reached for his door handle, but I wasn't going to let him escape this time.

"Oh, Mama said you liked to read. So do I. Could I tell you about my favorite book?"

"Some other time."

"Uncle Richard, why do you always say that? That was your answer when I asked you if you wanted to see my doll, feed the chickens with me, play with Marian, and spell words."

"I'm not good with children."

I spoke without thinking. "Well, either you're lying or Mama is. Because she told us all these wonderful stories about how you liked children, how you taught cabin boys to read, and played hoops in the yard with Aunt Susannah's children. I wish you'd be friendly because I'm…" I shut my lips tightly. I'd never tell him that.

"I'm not a good friend. I've made too many mistakes in the last years. It's better not to have friends because then you don't know what it's like to be lonely. Better to live in a world of command than to make friends and get hurt." He went inside his room and shut the door firmly.

Uncle Richard wouldn't be my friend. He didn't want to try trusting us. I went in my room, closed the door, flopped on the bed, and started crying. I had held back the tears when I said good-bye to Jane and Anna and when I saw these gray rocks so far from town and friends, but now those tears started and couldn't be stopped. The moments I had pushed away – the boys' irritating enthusiasm for our new home, Uncle Richard's aloofness, and even Mama's perfect acceptance – came back. I felt so alone. Nobody understood, cared, or even tried. And I'd never let anyone know how lonely I was.

I sat up, wiping the tears with determined frustration. Fine then, I decided. I'd keep my promises, I'd be the best lighthouse daughter I could be, and whenever I felt this way, I'd create my own world to hide my secret. At school, my teacher had said I was a good writer – good with poetry. That's it, I'll write poetry, I thought. And maybe I'll even be famous when I grow up. I scrubbed away the tear trails on my face. Instead of feeling sorry for myself, I would discover something new.

Surprisingly, my dear friends had even given me the way out of my loneliness. That lovely new notebook. I pulled it out of my trunk and snatched the pencil. Picking a simple word, I started crafting a list that rhymed. Poetry can't be all that hard, I thought. I'll just have to pick a topic or invent a story. There, I had it. A princess imprisoned in a tower near a crashing sea while her knight wandered the countryside looking for her. What should I name the princess? Never mind, that would come. For now, I focused on creating and lengthening my lists of rhymed words.

As I worked on this new project in my spare time, it pushed aside those frustrated feelings. I just ignored the memories, made attempts to get along better with my brothers now that their excitement about the new lighthouse had worn off, and didn't really try to interact with Uncle Richard. If he didn't want to be friends, why bother or make him unhappy?

Chapter 4

The March sun tried to peek through the drawn curtains, and I pulled the blue and white quilt over my head, unwilling to venture out of the warmth and coziness of bed. Mama opened the door, calling, "Good morning, Susan. It's time to be up." She was already dressed in her green plaid day dress and tied on her brown apron as she spoke.

"Yes, ma'am." I threw back the covers, half-squealing as my feet touched the cold, wood floor. The movements of dressing and making the bed warmed me. I drew back the curtains at the window and watched the tumbling waves.

There wasn't time to be idle; days started early for our family. There was always lots of work to be done. Not only did Mama have to manage the household, but it had to be kept to a standard of perfection. Just like Father and Uncle Richard had a duty to keep the light burning brightly and the lighthouse in good repair, I had a duty to assist Mama with the work of homemaking, but sometimes it seemed like never ending chores.

When I opened the door, Mattie danced in the hallway corner, playing with a folded paper. As I approached to see what she had, the cat darted through the cracked door into Uncle Richard's room. I picked up the folded paper and opened it. It was a sea chart, marked with shoals, islands, and a port city called Wilmington. I turned it over. Someone had written in ink: "Wilmington still safe." Whose was it? Where was Wilmington, and what was it safe from?

It wasn't mine, and I was pretty sure it wasn't Father's. Uncle Richard's? I decided to leave it where I found it and see what happened.

Downstairs, in the warm kitchen at the back of the house, Mama looked up from stirring the breakfast oatmeal and smiled at me. "Good morning, daughter. Please wait just a moment, and I will come into the other room and braid your hair. Go start brushing it."

I sat in front of the rocking chair, close to the low fire in the main room, and started brushing my hair, working through the little tangles and then making long sweeping strokes through the strands. Wilmington, Wilmington – I thought through all the state capitals I'd forced myself to learn in geography and shook my head. Where was that city?

"Two braids or one?" Mama asked, coming into the room, her wide skirt rustling.

"Two for today, please," I responded, waiting.

"Susan, dear, could you please come over here? I cannot sit in the rocking chair."

I giggled and asked, "Why not?" even though I knew the answer. Then I moved in front of the straight chair.

"I may be a sea captain's daughter," Mama replied, parting my hair and smoothing it with a comb, "and I married a man who loves the sea. But I get awfully seasick. Rocking chairs remind me too much of the movement of a boat. So straight-backed chairs only for me."

She fingered a worn spot on the back of my collar and tugged at one of my shortening sleeves. "We will need to make you a new dress before long. You are growing up too fast." She had worked as a seamstress before marrying Father and made beautiful clothes.

"Oh, what color will it be?"

"I don't know. We'll have to look at the fabrics I purchased and choose from those."

"Mama, where's Wilmington?" I asked, unable to forget the map as Mama's quick hands twisted my hair into smooth braids.

"Hmm..." She concentrated as she tied the ribbon on the first braid. The boys trooped in and interrupted our conversation. Jacob greeted the new day and Mama with enthusiasm while Paul complained softly about the cold floor until Mama suggested he should put on his shoes instead of carrying them. Upstairs, a faint wail announced Marian was awake.

In a quarter of an hour, Mama had us all at the breakfast table with washed faces, combed hair, and tied shoes. Marian lay on a blanket, kicking happily and making grunting baby sounds. The bowls of oatmeal were on the table, tickling our noses with aroma. Yet Father and Uncle Richard were missing. "I think just this once you can go ahead and start," Mama decided as Jacob and Paul mentioned for the third time they were hungry.

The door of the mud room – off the kitchen – banged open, and we could hear the men taking off their coats. Father had a big smile on his face as he took his place at the head of the table, and Uncle Richard looked a little awed.

"Did something happen, Father?" Jacob asked.

"Oh, something happened alright," he replied, concentrating on his oatmeal, though his mouth twitched into a smile. "I can't tell you until after you finish your breakfast."

Paul squirmed in his seat beside me. "Can we guess?"

"You can try."

I looked at Uncle Richard, hoping for a clue, but he shrugged, saying confidently, "You won't guess."

"You caught a big crab," Paul announced, but Father shook his head.

"You taught Uncle Richard how to swim," I said.

My uncle pretended to be indignant. "I can swim very well, young lady." I laughed at his comical expression.

"You saved a ship," Jacob guessed. After that, the guesses became sillier until Paul suggested they'd caught a sea monster. Then Father told us to finish eating.

When the last bite of oatmeal had been eaten and the table cleared, we stood expectantly while Father purposely drank his coffee slowly, watching us from the corner of his eye. He put down the cup and said quietly, "Go put on your coats, and meet me by the front door."

We put on our coats, following Father and Uncle Richard into the chilly morning. The boys hopped excitedly, and I skipped beside Father to keep up with his long stride. As we approached the shed, I heard a faint "maaa" inside. Then I knew. "Did Patches have her baby?" I eagerly asked.

Father opened the door, and we ran inside while the hens cackled in nervous surprise. A baby goat wriggled to its feet from a pile of hay and scampered over to Patches. It wobbled on little legs, turning to look back at us with a cute, curious expression. I wanted to hold it, and inwardly I wished Jane and Anna were here to see it too.

"It's brown!" Paul whispered to me. "Is it a boy or a girl?"

"Does it have a name yet?" I asked, kneeling in the straw when the kid came over to inspect us. I held out my hand and giggled as it nosed my fingers.

"No name yet, but it's a girl. Why don't you children think of a special name? Richard," Father said, "I need to get started on our morning chores. Would you stay with the children for a few minutes? Then they can come back to the house. Patches and her baby will need to rest." Uncle Richard nodded and seated himself against the wall.

The little goat had tumbled down contentedly, her head in my lap. I gently traced the white markings on her tiny face. "I like the name 'Clara.'" That was the name of Jane's porcelain doll, but of course I didn't say that.

Jacob leaned over and frowned. "That sounds like a cat or doll's name. Not a good name for a goat."

I tried several other names, but the boys kept shaking their heads at my suggestions, much to Uncle Richard's amusement. "Well, I give up," I announced, putting my hands on my hips. "You think of something."

"She's cute," Paul said, patting her back. "We could call her 'Pretty.'"

"That's silly," Jacob retorted.

"In Scotland," Uncle Richard said, "they might call her 'a bonnie thing' as their way of saying she was cute or pretty."

I smiled. "Bonnie. What do you think, boys? Patches and Bonnie?" My brothers cheered, and our baby goat finally had a name.

"How did you know that?" I asked, turning to Uncle Richard as Bonnie scrambled to her feet and stared at the boys.

"Know what, Susan?"

"About Scotland."

"Oh…" He paused, then continued. "I had friends in Scotland. I lived there for a little while too."

"You did?" This was something new that I hadn't heard, even in Mama's stories. "You never told us. Was it a nice place? Are the people friendly? Is it really as green as the story books say?"

He ignored my questions and motioned for us to come with him back to the house. "I don't talk about that time of my life."

"Was it not a good time?" I added, impulsively curious.

"I don't talk about it." His tone had a defensive edge.

I realized I had said too much. I tried to reach out and hold his hand, but he tucked it into his pocket. "I'm sorry. I shouldn't have asked. But thank you for helping us name Bonnie." Wordless, he walked away.

Then I realized it. Uncle Richard and I had something in common that we would not admit to each other or to the family. We both had secrets. Secrets that we were unwilling to share. Mine: loneliness. His? I didn't know.

Chapter 5

Was Wilmington in Scotland? The idea seemed logical. I thought about it as I started my disliked chore of the day: emptying the dirty water from the washbasins into a bucket, carrying it downstairs, and dumping it outside. There seemed to be something wonderfully mysterious about the discovered map. How did it get there? And why didn't Uncle Richard want to talk about Scotland?

I looked in the hallway corner. The map was gone, so I didn't have a chance to see it again. Who took it?

"Do you know where Wilmington is?" I asked Jacob as I went through the pantry to the back door.

"How would I know that?" he retorted, scowling at me. Jacob hated to dry the breakfast dishes, but it was one of his jobs.

Outside, I spotted Paul with his basket, gathering wood chips just inside the door of the storage shed. If Jacob doesn't know, Paul won't know, I reasoned.

After two trips up and down the stairs carrying the sloshing bucket, which seemed to get heavier each time, I finished. I did enjoy my second task: dusting and sweeping. Every morning I dusted the furniture in the main room and parlor and swept the kitchen, main room, and the hallways. Every third day Mama helped me, and we swept the parlor, storage rooms, and bedrooms and dusted every piece of furniture in the house. It amazed me how dirty everything got in a lighthouse. The sand, mud, and tiny rocks came in on our shoes. The coal stove and wood fires created smoke and ash. And then, there was the big light above our heads, creating a lot of smoke and soot every night.

Marian fussed that morning, and Mama asked me to hold the baby while she prepared the potatoes and fish to cook for the noon meal. I bounced my little sister and told her all about the baby goat while the boys started on their schoolwork, spelling a list of short words with alphabet tiles. When the kitchen work was finished for the morning, Mama took Marian and instructed me to get my lesson books.

At our Great Lake lighthouse, the school was only about a mile away. We had walked there with Jane and her older siblings until the snow got too deep. Here, at Herdman Point, the small town and schoolhouse were about five miles inland – too far to walk everyday, and we were too young to board with a family in town. Mama gave us our lessons to study and tested us on our new knowledge. I didn't mind studying, but I missed my friends. Jane and I had shared a desk, and we always ate lunch with Anna, which was the best time for whispering girlish secrets.

I looked over my slate filled with new arithmetic sums, opened my spelling book to see the list of long words, paged through my history, geography, and literature books, and frowned at my new column of vocabulary words. Usually, I liked my studies, but today all I wanted to know was about Uncle Richard's trip to Scotland and the location of Wilmington.

"Do I have penmanship today?" I asked Mama. She frequently had me copy a passage of Scripture or poetry to practice my writing. She shook her head and said we'd work on that tomorrow.

Jacob, Paul, and I sat in a row on the long bench in front of the dining table. Paul murmured softly to himself as he counted piles of dried beans to practice his numbers, and Jacob squeaked his chalk on the slate, making me shiver at the awful noise. I had finished my math, spelling, and history, and was trying to find ways to remember the capitals of the European countries when I felt something brush against my leg. I glanced down. "Mattie! You're getting friendly," I whispered. Cautiously, I reached down to pet her, but at the brush of my hand, she scampered away and hid in the parlor. Sighing, I continued reciting: London, Paris…

Later, at our noon meal – which we called dinner – I stabbed a bite of potato and looked across the table at Uncle Richard who was carefully cutting his fish. "Where is Wilmington? It's a port city, I think."

"North Carolina," Father responded, taking a sip of his tea. "Why?"

"Just wondering. Did you ever sail there?"

Father shook his head, and Jacob asked, "What about you, Uncle Richard?"

"A couple times." He stuttered on the words and put a bite in his mouth.

"Is it a pretty city?" Mama prompted.

"I guess so. It was probably damaged because of the war though. Most Southern port cities were." At the mention of the war, Mama didn't ask anymore.

"Were you in the war?" Paul piped up. "Were you a soldier?"

"I was not a soldier," Uncle Richard replied. "The war was destructive. I don't like to talk about it."

There's a lot he doesn't talk about, I thought. But at least I knew Wilmington was in North Carolina. I might be able to figure out the rest in time.

We usually had Bible reading after dinner. Father read a chapter and discussed the passage with us. Today, the section was the second chapter of Philippians, and Father emphasized a few verses. "Do all things without complaining and disputing, that you may become blameless and harmless, children of God without fault in the midst of a crooked and perverse generation, among whom you shine as lights in the world, holding fast to the word of life…" (Philippians 2:14-16). Work without complaining and shine a brilliant light, I thought. Lighthouse keeping is like living our faith: an endless effort and call.

The work continued after dinner with dishes and cleaning the table. Studies finished in the afternoon when Mama went over what I had learned to make sure I understood it well.

An early spring storm rolled in, darkening the room and forcing Father to illuminate the big light early; Uncle Richard took the first watch and sat patiently in the room below the lantern. The rain fell steady, and I leaned against the wall, tracing the water droplets as they ran down the window. Jacob pouted beside me. "I wanted to play with Bonnie," he said.

"She's very little," Father said, coming into the main room and finding his book. "When the storm ends in a day or two, she will be stronger and better able to play with you."

While Marian took her nap and the boys drew pictures on their slates, Mama beckoned me to follow her into the parlor. "I have been thinking it's time for you to start a sampler."

"A sampler, Mama? You mean like the pretty embroidery pieces you made when you were a girl and which decorate our house now?" I glanced at the framed embroidered basket of flowers hanging on the parlor wall. "Do you really think I can?" Anna's older sister had made beautiful samplers and always implied it was a pastime for "big girls." Maybe I was finally growing up!

"Yes, it's a good way for a girl to learn and perfect her fancy sewing skills. I have some suitable fabric here and plenty of brightly colored thread. Would you like to choose a proverb or quote to stitch? You can also think about what you would like to put around it."

"I don't know what I should choose," I admitted.

"Well, choose something that is important to you. Think about it for a day or two, and then I will help you prepare the fabric."

I knelt on the floor by the big sewing basket, fingering the threads. I loved the shades of blue. It reminded me of the lake. What could I say in my sewing? I wondered. What was important to me? I liked flowers, birds, sea shells, and some challenges of living in a lighthouse. I had heard something recently, a phrase or saying I had liked. What was it? Mama had said I had time to think about it. Shrugging, I would decide soon, but not now.

It was quiet in the main room, everyone busy with their own projects. Uncle Richard was still on watch. Father had been reading in his rocking chair, but now the book lay in his lap, his head rested back, and he snored a little. The boys were still drawing, and Mama darned stockings.

"Mama," I said, "can I help you with anything?"

"No, I don't think so right now," she replied, pausing in her work.

"Then may I go up to my room to read? I will keep thinking about the sampler too."

She nodded, and I climbed upstairs, taking the next paper Mama had said I could read. I flopped on my bed, lying toward the window for light.

At the top of the page, it said January 1865. Smoothing the wrinkles, I first looked for the poetry column. I'd found wonderful patriotic poetry in some of the papers and enjoyed examining how the stories about American heroes had been written. Pretty soon, I'd finish my lists of rhyming words, and I was already imagining a lively story about a princess in need of rescue.

Unfortunately, there wasn't a poem in this copy. On the back page was a shocking report about some bad Confederate raiders. I didn't want to read that and turned to the front page. The headline caught my eye. A fort – Fort Fisher – had been captured by Union soldiers. The port of Wilmington closed, meaning no ships could go in or out. The article explained that Wilmington had been an important port for blockade runners, but it didn't explain what those were.

What had been written on that map? Something about safety. Safety from what? And was it Father's or Uncle Richard's? Confused, I pushed the paper onto the floor and tried to think about something else.

I thought of Jane and Anna. Were they starting samplers too? I wished I could write them a letter, but it would be a while before the inspector would come to bring and take our mail or someone would go to town. Leaning my chin on my folded hands, I looked at my doll, sitting forlornly on the trunk and remembered the tea parties at the shore, in our woodland playhouse, or in front of the cozy indoor fire when we'd all pretended to be fine, grown-up ladies. If only they were here, or I was there…

"Stop it!" I said aloud. "I'm only making myself feel bad. I'm not going to feel sorry for myself. I had just about forgotten to be lonely, and now I'm lying here remembering it all. That's stupid…"

I turned over and stared at the ceiling. Poetry. I really should work on a story about that princess. If I closed my eyes, could I imagine I was the princess, imprisoned in a cold tower? I tried. But it didn't work. Not when I knew that below there was a cheerful fire and my loving family. After a while, I felt disappointed. I couldn't think of anything to write about today. And I kept wondering what Wilmington, North Carolina, looked like. What had the war really done?

Chapter 6

I forgot to wonder about ruined cities when I went downstairs to help Mama with supper. The wind whipped the rain against the windows, but it was warm in the main room. Uncle Richard came in, slicking back his wet hair. "Are the goats doing good?" Jacob asked. "Did you give them supper?" Our uncle reported Patches and Bonnie were fine, and Bonnie wasn't even scared of the storm.

Father was at his turn at light watch, and the rest of us ate supper. Afterwards, when the supper dishes were washed and put away, Mama and I closed the kitchen door and joined the boys and Uncle Richard near the fire. Jacob and Paul sat on either side of Uncle Richard's chair, watching him carve a piece of driftwood. I brought Mama's bag of fabric strips and sat beside her; we were braiding the long, thin lengths of fabric to make a rug for my room.

"We should tell Uncle Richard a story," Jacob said. "A story with lots of adventure." He thought for a moment, "We could tell him about lighthouses. Like Father tells us."

Marian started crying upstairs, and Mama went to check on her, leaving us alone with Uncle Richard.

"Do you know when the first lighthouse was built in America?" Jacob asked, tugging on Uncle Richard's foot.

"Tell him, Susan! Tell him!" Paul insisted.

"The first lighthouse that we know of in America guarded Boston Harbor." I recited the fact easily and continued braiding the strips of fabric.

"And? What about the British?" Jacob prompted, crawling over to my chair.

"Well, Father says during America's first war with Britain – the one when we were fighting for independence – the British blew up the light tower to darken the shores, but after the war, it was repaired, and the light still shines today."

"And were there lots of lighthouses back then? When George Washington was president?" Jacob prompted, looking at Uncle Richard to make sure he was paying attention.

I sighed, not pleased about reciting facts and not sure that Uncle appreciated the history lesson. "No, not really," I said, repeating what Father had explained to us on many occasions. "It wasn't until around the 1820's and 1830's that the government started building many lighthouses. A man named Stephen Pleasonton oversaw the lighthouses and the keepers during that time. He was enthusiastic about building new lighthouses and running those establishments on a very tight budget." I hoped that would be enough details to satisfy my brothers.

"Were people happy about all the new lighthouses?" Uncle Richard asked, taking an interest for the first time in the conversation.

"That's the exciting part," Paul said. "Do you know about wreckers? Oh, let's go ask Father to tell you all about it."

I felt hurt that I wasn't telling the story entertainingly but also happy to give up the role of evening storyteller. The boys insisted that we all go up to the watchroom and ask Father to finish the story. And finish it properly!

We trooped upstairs, the boys first, leading Uncle Richard who still seemed mostly indifferent to the tale. I followed behind. There wasn't room in the watchroom for all of us, so the boys sat on the floor, Uncle Richard sat on the top stair, and I stood against the staircase wall. Once we were settled, Father agreed to the boys' clamorous request to finish the lighthouse stories.

"Wreckers. Well, you got pretty far in the history with Susan Rose telling. Alright, the new lighthouses pleased the ship captains and lighthouse keepers. But other folks weren't so pleased. You see, in parts of the country, particularly the Southern region, some people made a living from ship wrecks. They would salvage and sell the cargo. Some of these "wreckers" – as they were sometimes called – developed ways of luring ships onto shoals or beaches."

"Like pirates on shore!" Paul exclaimed. He shivered.

"That's awful," I exclaimed, making an appropriate response when Jacob looked to see my reaction.

"Yes. The lighthouses changed that. They became true and steady beacons, instructing ships to steer away from the danger. Dark shores are dangerous. Evil loves darkness, but light points the true way to safety."

After talking about lighthouses and listening to Father's stories, I realized what I wanted to put on my sampler. A lighthouse. Perhaps with a Scripture verse about light.

"Is Mr. Pleasonton still in charge of the lighthouses?" Uncle Richard asked. "Susan had mentioned his work."

"No, in 1852 the United States Lighthouse Board was established. Mr. Pleasonton had done a lot of good for the American coastlines, but because he was so thrifty, he didn't want to upgrade to better equipment – like the Fresnel lens. Now the Lighthouse Board is in charge, and their inspectors make sure the keepers attend to the lights properly and don't waste supplies or neglect duties."

"Like Inspector Milton?" Paul questioned.

"Yes, exactly. His job is to make sure we are keeping our light bright, our house clean, our accounts in order."

"And, if we don't, we get dismissed?"

"Yes," Father said. "There have been many keepers through the decades who have been dismissed, but there have been many more who have been loyal to their lights and dedicated to their work of saving lives."

Loyal, I thought. What exactly does that word mean? I could spell it, but I wondered about the definition. I decided to look it up later; it might be the perfect way to describe a knight in shining armor in poetry.

The steady, bright flashes from the light overhead, cast shadows in the cozy watchroom. "Some keepers have resisted attacks. Some have gone through extreme hardship and rough seas to save shipwrecked crews. And – in more recent circumstances – some have hidden their lenses and equipment to save it."

"When was that, Father?" I asked, sitting down on one of the stair steps.

"During the war," he said briefly and then continued. "Most of the lighthouses on the Southern coast were captured by the Rebels. Some lenses were used for target practice. Lighthouse towers were shot by cannons, and the majority of the lightkeepers fled. Almost the entire Southern coastline was dark, I'm told."

"Tell us more," Jacob begged eagerly.

"I wish I could," Father admitted, "but I don't know much beyond those facts right now. Maybe later we will learn more."

"Do you know any stories about lighthouses in the war?" Jacob asked, turning to Uncle Richard.

"Dark coastlines are treacherous," he replied simply. "No, I don't have any particular stories about lighthouses."

"Oh, but do you have a good war story?" Paul suggested. "We like exciting stories!"

Uncle Richard shook his head and leaned back as if looking for a shadow to hide his face. "I do not have any stories that I wish to tell."

I glanced at him, surprised at the emptiness that had crept into his tone. I'd never seen a ruined city, but something in his tone made me picture what I thought it must look like. Broken down, gloomy, filled with hidden memories. I shivered – unexplainably the shadows of war seemed close in that moment, but they retreated in the light of Father's words.

"I need to go up and check the lamp wicks. There's been a change in the brightness. Susan Rose, boys, it's chilly up here. Why don't you go back downstairs? Strike up a rousing song on the way down." The words of an appropriate sea chantey Father had taught us resounded in the hallways as we led the way downstairs, Uncle Richard following. As we snickered at the silly words, that dark feeling disappeared completely.

"Do you know any new songs to teach us, Uncle Richard?" I asked, after we had resettled in the main room and sung several of our favorites, entertaining Mama and Marian.

"Oh, I don't know that it's new, but there is a song I could sing for you. Someone taught it to me a few years ago," he replied quietly, shifting in his chair.

"Sing it, sing it," Paul chanted. Uncle Richard cleared his throat, and we waited, expecting a lively tune. Instead, he sang simple words and a pleasing melody:

Beautiful dreamer, wake unto me,
Starlight and dewdrops are waiting for thee;
Sounds of the rude world, heard in the day,
Lull'd by the moonlight have all passed away!
Beautiful dreamer, queen of my song,

List while I woo thee with soft melody;
Gone are the cares of life's busy throng,
Beautiful dreamer, awake unto me!
Beautiful dreamer, awake unto me!

He sang toward the window where the light from the lantern above us played in the darkness. Mother paused in her braiding and listened, watching her brother. I thought he sang to someone who wasn't there. Like he was looking – or waiting – for someone to come back.

"That was lovely, Richard. It's been too long since I've heard you sing." Mama studied her work. "Where did you learn that song?"

"It's an American song by Foster, but I learned it while I was in Scotland."

"Richard," Mama looked at him gently, "what were you doing in Scotland?"

"I told you the other evening, Harriet. Working in a chandlery store. Selling ropes, navigation equipment, lanterns, mops, and other items needed on ships." He crossed his arms defensively, countering, "Do you think I'm lying?"

"I don't know what to think. That's why I'm asking."

He uncrossed his arms and cleared his throat as if preparing to speak, then crossed his arms again and stood up. "Never mind. I don't have anything to say." He walked away from the lamplight into the dark entrance hall, and we heard his retreating footsteps on the stairs.

Mama instructed the boys to put away their few scattered toys from earlier in the day and to get ready for bed. I had just sewn new long strips to braid, and Mama said I could finish them if I worked quickly.

I thought about asking Mama about Uncle Richard and what she thought, but before I decided on my question, she said quietly, "Do you miss your friends?"

I leaned closer to the braiding as if inspecting it in the dim light. I wouldn't lie to Mama, but I didn't want to tell her. "I'm going to write some poetry in that nice notebook they gave me," I announced.

"Poetry?" Mama asked, surprised. "That is a new interest for you. What inspired this?"

"Just something I want to try. Epic poetry. Does that sound exciting?" I paused, considering. "What does 'epic' really mean?"

Mama laughed. "I think in this case it means a long, famous poem. It does sound like an exciting idea, and I will look forward to reading your epic poetry."

"Well, it might be a while before I have a really, really good poem."

"That's alright," Mama laughed. "I can wait. I'm glad you have a new interest."

As I clipped the end of my braided cloth for the evening, I struggled, wanting to tell Mama how much I missed Jane and Anna and how writing poetry was just a way to distract my thoughts. But when I glanced at her, she looked so calm, happy, and content that I thought she would somehow think less of me if she knew I wasn't as strong inside as I was outwardly busy. A weight pressed in my chest, and my throat felt tight.

Mama gave me a hug, and when she kissed my cheek, I nearly broke my promise not to talk or think about being lonely. I ran through the darkness to my room, undressed quickly, and sank into bed, hiding the tears.

Chapter 7

Loyal – true to plighted faith, duty, or love; not treacherous
I shook my head. It was a good word, but the printed words on the dictionary page seemed cold. What did loyalty really mean? What did it look like in real life? I closed the book and slid it back on the shelf in the parlor.

Thoughtfully, I reached for my notebook and read through the long lists of rhymed words and the optional names for the princess. Matilda, Cornelia, Anne, Margaret, Catherine, Rosemarie… I didn't know which one to choose, and I was getting tired of thinking of names. I wanted to be writing, creating.

Father sat at the desk in the corner, his pen making faint scratchy sounds as he wrote in the logbook for the day. I went, stood beside him, and waited quietly until he stabbed a period and glanced up at me.

"Can you help me think of some names? I'm trying to write a poem about a princess, but I can't think of the right name."

"Mama said you were trying your hand at poetry," he said with an approving smile. "As for names, I think I used my stock of good names on my children."

"Tell me again how I got my name," I begged.

"Well," he looked at me with a gentle smile as if remembering something extra special, "you were born on the day a fierce storm broke. You and the sunlight came at the same time. For several months before you were born, I'd been teasing Mama that we would name you after one of my whaling ships, and she insisted we would not. You were going to be named after one of your grandmothers or aunts. So I gave in and announced that I liked the name 'Susannah.' So we called you Susannah Rose Arnold. Rose – like the early summer flowers blooming in our seaside garden."

"And then?" I wriggled in anticipation.

"Oh, one day an officer from the first ship I sailed on came by, and we were reminiscing about the old days. And Mama found out that my first ship was the *Susan Rose*."

"Was she unhappy?" I already knew the answer.

"No. She teased me but said I was a clever man." He looked proud as he hugged me. "I loved my first ship, but I definitely love my Susan Rose best."

"What were your other ships, Father? Did you name the boys after them?"

"No." He gave a short laugh. "*Hatchet, Icewall*, and *Cousin Jasper*. Shall you name the prince after those ships?" He chucked me playfully under the chin.

"I don't think so. 'Sir Icewall' doesn't sound very gallant. Besides I need a princess name."

Father stood up. "While you're thinking of that wonderful name, do you want to help me check the traps down by the dock?" I nodded and ran to put on my coat; the early spring air was still chilly.

"Are there any whales here?" I asked as we descended the path.

"Not likely. You won't see whales here, Susan Rose. They've been hunted for too many years. I'm afraid they're nearly gone, at least along our coast." There was sadness in his voice. "Sometimes I wish I'd never done it, but other times I'm glad I did."

"Did what, Father?" I asked, looking up at him.

"You know. I worked on a whaling ship…before I married your mother. There is nothing comparable to the sea lashed by a fighting whale. Nothing so powerful as a mighty fluke crashing down near the little boats. Nowhere except at sea – fighting nature and the largest animals on earth – do you realize how small man must be in God's eyes."

"Why did you do it?"

Father didn't answer immediately, preoccupied pulling in the lobster traps from the deep water beneath the dock to see if we'd caught anything good and then tossing the empty trap back.

"Why did we do it?" he repeated, questioningly, pulling in the second line. "For the money, to be blunt. Whale oil is valuable. Whalebone too. It is also part of the society I grew up in – New Bedford – the whaling capital of America. My family was not wealthy. It was expected that the boys would go to sea." He sighed. "I do think the whales have been hunted too much. I would like to point out a spout or a breaching whale to you, but it is unlikely you will ever see one, especially so close to shore."

"Got one!" I squealed as the trap surfaced and an angry lobster snapped his claw through an opening.

"We got two," Father corrected. "Just what Mama wanted to make soup. I suppose we'll get more lobsters regularly when it gets warmer and they head for the shallower waters." He pulled a sack from his coat pocket and carefully plopped the unhappy lobsters inside, then pushed the empty trap back into the water.

"What made you stop whaling?" I asked as we started back up the path.

"A very profitable voyage, an injury, and Miss Bates," he answered, grinning.

"Miss Bates? That must've been Mama!" I exclaimed. "Did you know Uncle Richard then too?"

"It was Mama. No, I did not meet Uncle Richard at that time. I was a second mate on a whaling ship... You see, one day we were out in the small boats chasing a whale, and the long and short of it was, the whale got us. I was knocked unconscious, and when I came to, I'd nearly drowned and had a badly broken arm. That put things in perspective for me. I'd already been courting Miss Bates, and she was waiting for me to come home for a wedding. I figured I'd come close enough to dying, and if I wanted a family, it might be a good idea to find a safer job, and I had enough money to establish a household. I took a position as a lightkeeper. They were happy to hire me because I knew the weather, the sea, and the importance of shore lights."

I stopped suddenly. A new brilliant idea in my mind. "Do you think Uncle Richard would be happier if he met a nice lady and got married?"

"That's an idea," Father replied, smirking. "But let Uncle Richard figure that out on his own."

A plan had formed in my mind by the time we reached the house. It couldn't hurt anything to find out if Uncle Richard liked a lady. Maybe he was even writing her letters. What if that was his big secret? No, maybe not, I reasoned; after all, a secret like that should make him happy. Oh, but maybe the lady had rejected him. In that case, I could tell Mama, and she could write the lady a letter and tell her how sad Uncle Richard was and then…

I couldn't resist the opportunity to ask and thought I'd found a good way. If I asked Uncle Richard what to name the princess in my poem, then maybe I would get a clue from his answer. "Do you know where Uncle Richard is?" I asked Father, after we showed the wriggly lobsters to Mama and the boys.

"Finishing the brass polishing in the storage room, I think. Don't go pestering him with questions," Father said, wagging his finger at me as if he knew what I wanted to ask my uncle. Would it qualify as pestering to ask for a suggestion? I wondered as I retrieved my notebook and headed to the storage room.

Uncle Richard leaned against the work bench, rubbing the brass work of the lightkeeping tools until it glowed brightly. Each tool was supposed to be shiny and without soot, dirt, or fingerprints; the inspector took special note of the shiny brass each time he came. Uncle seemed preoccupied, but he looked up when I came in and tilted the brass in his hand so I could see my reflection. I made a silly face; he smiled and started polishing again.

I leaned against a barrel and looked up at him. "I'm sorry for asking too many questions these last few weeks," I started. "I guess I know now you prefer quiet." He made an odd expression. "So I won't talk too long. But I'm doing some writing, and I was wondering if you might have some ideas."

"I'm not a writer. I'm a seaman who's been cast ashore."

"Oh, I just need an opinion." Laying my notebook on a nearby barrel, I opened to the page of name choices, asking Uncle Richard if he thought one name would be particularly nice. When he said he didn't have any preferences, I added, "I was liking 'Margaret.' Princess Margaret sounds important, don't you think?"

Uncle Richard's busy hands stilled mid-motion. His blue eyes became like stone, and he set his jaw. He took a deep breath and said quietly. "I do not have any particular preference for a name, but do not use the name Margaret. That name is

too beautiful, too precious. Do not use the name Margaret."
He abruptly laid down the brass work and cloth, turning away
from me and looking out the window.

I wanted to ask him why. But he stood so straight and
immovable, staring at something faraway. I went out, afraid
to speak and unsure what he meant. Why would a simple
name bother him so much? I couldn't understand that look.
No sorrow, no joy, no longing – just a hollow, emotionless
expression. Exactly the type of empty sadness I didn't want,
and all the more reason to write poetry.

The next day, after chores, schoolwork, and sewing, I
went to the watchroom to work on my first epic poem. There,
sitting in front of the ladder was Mattie. I sat down and spoke
to her, extending my hand toward her. Mattie's nose twitched
curiously, and her eyes shifted fearfully. "It's alright," I crooned
softly. She took a hesitating step forward and waited. Then
her tail waved like a friendly flag, and Mattie came close and
pressed against my knee.

"Mattie, how nice to meet you," I whispered, gently
stroking her soft fur. She purred happily. When I stood up and
made my way to the ladder, the calico cat followed, sprang up
on the low window sill, and stared at me.

Encouraged by this new friendship, I opened my notebook
and surprisingly the words and rhyming flowed smoothly.
When I had filled several pages with inspired writing, I went
back and read my work. The account of a lost princess named
Rosemarie who had been kidnapped and imprisoned on an
island off the coast of France. She spent her days braiding

sheets into a rope and hoping to escape, but alas she could not swim. At that point, I ran out of ideas. How was the prince going to rescue her?

Ah, I had it! The handsome, loyal prince made a pact with a large whale which took him to the island castle, allowing him to rescue the princess, and they became the king and queen of the sea. A genius idea and my first epic poem.

I read the five page poem to Mattie, who listened in wide-eyed amazement to my story-telling skill. "This is it," I whispered to my new companion. "I've written it! I don't want to show Father and Mama until I have a collection, but I have to share it with someone." I thought for a moment. "Uncle Richard," I said aloud.

"Niece Susan," he said gravely, just before I saw him on the stairs.

"Oh, you startled me!" I turned the closed notebook three times in my hands, wondering if he would care, if he would think I was silly, or if he would just find my writing and ideas annoying.

Uncle Richard looked at me and raised his eyebrows expectantly. "I don't think I've ever seen you at a loss for words. Was there something you wanted to tell me?"

Finally, I blurted out the news. "I've been writing epic poetry. I really want to wait and surprise my parents, but I need an opinion. Can I read it to you?"

"Poetry?" Uncle Richard asked. "I do enjoy a good poem. Let's hear it." He sat down on the top stair step and gave me his full attention.

I read the five pages in the most thrilling tone I could manage. When I finished, he was leaning against the wall, trying not to smile. I took that as a good sign. "What did you think?"

"It's quite the story," he replied in a noncommittal way.

"Then you think I should share it with Mama and Father and maybe even send it to a publisher?"

He sighed and crossed his arms. "Susan, do you think that story could possibly happen?"

"Well…no," I admitted, after considering the bargain with the whale. "But epic poetry doesn't have to be real, does it?"

"Maybe not. But if it couldn't have really happened, then it must convey something powerful and moving to make it worthwhile."

"So you think it's bad?" I asked, closing the book and holding it protectively.

Uncle Richard uncrossed his arms, and his expression softened. "Why are you writing, Susan?" I couldn't answer that and looked out the window. "Why do you really want to write?" he asked again.

I studied my shoelaces, then mumbled. "Why don't you tell us about your past?"

"What was that?" Uncle Richard questioned. A commanding tone crept into his voice.

I couldn't tell him that I wrote to escape the loneliness and my longing to see other girls my own age. That it was a way to keep my mind busy. "I guess we all have our secrets," I replied, turning the notebook in my hands again.

He sighed and said sincerely, "You might not get that piece published. But you should keep writing."

I swallowed my sadness and said, "So what do you really think about my poetry?"

"I think you have big ideas but no concept of reality." He looked down at his restless hands. "The prince cannot always save the princess."

"Thank you...for your honest opinion," I choked out the words, willing myself not to cry.

"I came for my pocket knife. Could you hand it to me?"

I picked up the knife from the chair, gave it to him, and he disappeared down the stairs.

Mattie – my faithful admirer – lounged in the window sill, watching me from narrowed eyes. I read the poem again for her benefit. It was good, I told myself. It was imaginative. There was conflict. But it had a happy ending. Why did my uncle dislike happy endings? Fine, I decided, I'll write a weepy poem, and everybody will die, and then he'll like it.

Frustrated, I dropped my pencil, and it rolled across the board floor. I stared out the window, watching the restless waves.

Chapter 8

"It's spring! It's spring!" Paul shouted as he ran in from the yard when Mama called the boys to dinner.

"The weather is finally getting a little warmer," Jacob announced. "It's nice in the sun today. Bonnie's getting bigger. She tried to push me over."

"And the chickens are happy," Paul added as he climbed onto the bench at the table.

I couldn't wait to go outside. I had stayed in to help Mama finish the meal preparations, but the pleasant sunshine and friendly sea beckoned to me. Inwardly, I had to admit: even at the old lighthouse on the lake, the late April days had never seemed this beautiful and inviting.

"I've been thinking about a garden," Mama said, looking at Father across the dinner table. "Mrs. Vendal gave me those seeds, remember? And I found some seed potatoes too. It would be nice to have fresh vegetables in the summer and autumn."

"And flowers too, Mama?" I asked, trying to remember if there were flower seeds in the package. She nodded.

"I think we should be able to manage that," Father said, cutting a slice of bread from the warm loaf on the table. "We have enough fresh water in the cistern, so we won't need to worry, even if we need to hand water our plants."

"Yes, but where will the plants actually grow?" Uncle Richard spoke up. "There must be a solution."

"But we have lots of sunshine and water," Jacob reasoned. "Why won't they grow?"

Father smiled. "Plants need good soil, too, and we're basically living on rocks. Thus, the roots won't go down, and the plants will die."

"But Mama wants a garden," Paul reminded him, ever thoughtful of his mother's wishes.

"Yes, and she will have a garden. There might be a patch of good soil a little farther back on this outcropping. Shall we take a walk after dinner and see?"

We made a family outing of the expedition. Mama, carrying Marian, walked beside Father. We children ran and chased each other, laughing and enjoying the day. Uncle Richard stayed at the lighthouse and promised to come see the garden place if we found one.

As we walked, I thought about a new poetic idea: a flower princess outsmarting a wicked dragon who wanted to destroy her garden. It had been a couple weeks since my disagreement with Uncle Richard about poetry, but oddly, it had somehow formed a bond between us. A single common interest. An interest related to our separate secrets? I couldn't help wondering.

We weren't exactly friends – definitely not like I was friends with Jane and Anna – but he had surprised me a week after our disagreement by asking if I had written any more poems. I had shared a couple of my latest attempts with him. He didn't comment much, though he seemed pleased and flattered to be my quiet, not-very-opinionated confidant. I couldn't wait for the day he thought a poem was perfect. Then – I'd decided – I would share it with Mama and Father.

At quite a distance from the lighthouse, we still had not found the right place for a garden, and we returned slowly, feeling a little sad. "No suitable ground?" Uncle Richard asked, coming out of the storage shed and wiping his dusty hands on his trousers.

"I'm afraid not." Mama shook her head, disappointed.

"We could build garden boxes," my uncle suggested to Father. "And there are some barrels and extra wood left behind by the former keepers that are not inventoried in the official supply list. We could cut the barrels and plant the flowers inside. We'd just need to haul some good soil from inland. What do you think?"

"Brilliant!" Father exclaimed, clapping Uncle Richard on the shoulder. "I can't believe I didn't think of that myself. We could put the garden boxes on the inland side, at the back of the lighthouse in the large empty space between the house and stable shed. Then the plants might get a little protection from the wind. What do you think, Harriet?" he asked, turning to Mama.

She smiled brightly. "I think it's a lovely idea, Samuel."

During the next few days, the saw rasped and the hammers pounded as Father and Uncle Richard spent their spare time sawing two of the barrels in half and building rectangular frames out of the boards. We would have four narrow garden boxes and six garden barrels. Each evening the boys reported how many nails they had pounded. Mama and I looked through the seed packets and decided what we would plant in each container.

Building the boxes was work for the men and boys. Inside, I got to keep my hands clean and watched them work as I pulled the colored thread through the coarse linen of my sampler. For the last couple weeks, I had faithfully stitched for a little while each afternoon. Today, I would complete the lighthouse which showed my new sewing skills – satin, cross, and stem stitches. On the right side of the sampler, I had penciled the Scripture verse from the Book of Genesis, "Let there be light," and would begin stitching that next week. Eventually, I would add my name and the year along the water's horizontal line.

Beside me, Mama frowned, concentrating on the even gathers in a skirt. Last week we had picked a salmon pink calico from the box of fabrics Mama had purchased before we came to the lighthouse. In the afternoons, she had been working on my new dress, and I couldn't wait to try it on!

Glancing out the window, I spotted Father, Uncle Richard, and the boys rolling a closed barrel from the edge of the trees, along the rough path. Curious, I watched. When they pried off the lid near the garden boxes and started scooping out soil, I realized what they were doing – bringing good dirt for our planter beds. Though it was a comical looking way to bring the soil, it seemed to work well.

After a few days of this creative hauling, the garden boxes and barrels were filled and ready for planting, and the following afternoon, Mama put on her straw hat and invited us to help her in the garden. While Marian sat on a small quilt nearby, Jacob, Paul, and I poked the seeds into the warm earth. The vegetables were planted in the boxes and in two of the barrels. Two other barrels got flower seeds, and Mama had had the men move the last two barrels to the front of the lighthouse – facing the sea – and we planted the prettiest flowers there.

Uncle Richard joined us. "Can I help?" Mama poured a packet of seeds into his hand.

"Do you like flowers?" Paul asked, patting Uncle Richard's sleeve with his dirty hand.

"They're pretty." He paused and flicked the clumps of dirt off his sleeve.

"We had flowers at our lighthouse on the lake. A big garden in the ground," I said, "with a fence around it to try to keep the rabbits out."

"Do you remember the day you, Anna, and Jane picked all the sweet pea blossoms and made flower wreaths, Susan?" Mama asked.

"Yes, I remember," I mumbled, trying not to recall Jane's laughter and Anna's songs as we had danced along the shore.

"I picked flowers for Mama," Jacob remembered.

Mama smiled at him. "That was so thoughtful of you." She stood up and put Marian back on the center of the large quilt. My little sister wasn't quite crawling yet, but she could inch, wriggle, roll, and scoot just about anywhere; Mama said she'd start trying to crawl soon.

"Did you ever take flowers to anyone, Uncle Richard?" I asked, thinking it might be a way to find out if Uncle liked anyone. Liked anyone enough to get married!

He scooped the dirt into a mound and buried the squash seeds. "Maybe flowers for my mother when I was little? In a market in Scotland, there was a cart that sold fresh flowers. They were beautiful. Daisies were...a favorite."

"Did you buy any?" Jacob asked.

"And in the summer on the hills, the wild heather bloomed. It's purple. I looked and looked for white heather. It's rare but said to be lucky for brides. And I wanted to see some."

Mama and I looked at each other across the planter boxes. "To see brides or white heather?" Mama teased. I thought she looked for answers too.

Uncle Richard rolled his eyes. "Oh, never mind, Harriet. You imagine too much."

"Do I?"

He looked behind him quickly, then finished planting the seeds. "I'll go in. I think I forgot to write something in the records."

"Do you think Uncle Richard is going to get married?" I whispered to Mama.

"Why wouldn't he tell us?"

"All I know," I answered, "is he feels funny about the name 'Margaret.'" Mama straightened and looked toward the house, just as Uncle Richard closed the door. I patted the dirt lightly over the flower seeds, wondering how long it would take for them to sprout and reveal their colorful blossoms.

When we had finished the planting and washed our hands, we sat on the front steps, eating cookies Mama had baked for a special treat. Father and Uncle Richard joined us. It was a calm day; we saw a few ships sailing at a safe distance from the rocks. The ships made me think of Father's stories, and I remembered Uncle Richard had also sailed. I turned to him. "Uncle Richard?"

"Niece Susan," he replied, playfully tugging the end of my braid.

"Could you tell us about some of the ships you sailed on?"

"Oh, there's not that much to tell. Unlike your father who was in the whaling industry, I sailed on merchant ships. After my father's financial losses in whaling, he determined that his youngest son was not going to be involved in that business. So I got started as a cabin boy on a merchant vessel."

"At age eleven," Mama murmured, as if remembering an unhappy day.

"What was its name?" Jacob asked, referring to the ship.

"*Seasprite*. *Seasprite* was the first, then *Hampton* and *Fair Lily*. I eventually became a ship's officer or mate."

"During the war, Father didn't have to go fight for either side because he was lightkeeper in the north. What about you?" I questioned.

Uncle Richard brushed cookie crumbs off his shirt and said lightly, "Oh, I left America during the war. When I came back to our native shores, the ship I was aboard got wrecked in a bad storm. I made my way to New York, but not finding a sailing position, I went to Lake Michigan and was hired by a merchant company to captain one of their ships. That was the *Esther*. I lost her in a terrible storm, but the crew and I escaped in one of the small boats. Having lost two ships, I began to think I am bad luck or was unskilled."

"Well, I think you know a lot about sailing," I said, trying to cheer him. "So it couldn't be bad luck, could it?" Uncle Richard smiled briefly but did not look convinced.

"What year did you come back?" Father asked.

"1864."

Just as Jacob opened his mouth to start asking questions, Uncle Richard got up, saying, "The sun will be on the horizon soon. I will go make sure the lamps are still ready." He went away, taking the answers to all our questions with him.

"The war ended in 1865, Harriet," Father said. "Do you really think he was working in a chandlery shop in Scotland during the war? How does that connect with his New Bedford bred patriotism that you've been championing?"

"What are you suggesting?" Mama retorted. "I don't know any more about this than you. We both made the decision to ask him to live with us and be the assistant keeper."

"I know." He lowered his voice. "But do you think he's…" Father didn't finish his sentence, but I knew the word: lying.

Chapter 9

"Goodness gracious," Mama remarked one morning as she washed the dishes and I dried them. "It's the twentieth of May already."

"Wait 'til you see how tall the little plants are this morning," Jacob announced, running inside after helping Father feed the animals.

Paul went to Mama with a happy smile on his face. "Look what I found for you!"

Mama set down the basin of dishwater she was preparing to take outside and turned to her youngest son. "Oh, that's lovely!"

"Don't look, Susan," he ordered. "Here's one for you too!" Paul handed me a pretty shell. "I found it on the beach when Father went down to check the lobster traps."

"Thank you. I'll put it on the windowsill in my room so I'll see it every morning." I held the shell up to my ear, listening to the sea-like murmur captured by it. An idea! Something new for poetry…

"Can I tell you a secret?" Paul asked. I nodded, and he pulled me down so he could whisper in my ear. I had no idea what he said and still didn't after the second time. We went into the parlor, and in a voice barely above a whisper, he said, "Uncle Richard is teaching me how to whistle."

"That's a secret?"

"Oh, yes! But not for long. Don't tell anyone." He pointed his finger at me to emphasize and repeated, "Anyone." Hiding my giggles from him, I went back into the main room. If only all secrets were so small and simple.

That day it seemed like nothing went smoothly. Father and Uncle Richard had spent the previous week cleaning the rain gutters and fixing the roof – normal lighthouse tasks at the change of seasons. Today, they planned to start painting the wooden trim on the outside of the lighthouse; it was a job that needed to be done, and it would please Inspector Milton when he arrived sometime during the summer. Unfortunately, painting didn't get very far because the wooden ladder split; they cobbled it back together but decided to paint the lower story door and window frames after hauling water for Mama.

It was wash day for Mama and I, and it would be a long while before I had time to write. I collected the dirty laundry for my first task in the day's work and sorted it while Mama heated the water and prepared the tubs. I made a couple trips up and down the stairs and only had one room left.

"Uncle Richard," I called, leaning out my bedroom window, "can I go in your room to get the laundry? Mama needs it."

He paused in his painting and the slowly whistled rendition of "Beautiful Dreamer," replying, "Yes, Susan. It's all in a pile at the foot of my bed."

I opened the door to Uncle Richard's room, and there, just as he had said, was the pile of laundry. The sparse and plain room contained a bed covered with a light blue woolen blanket, small bookshelf lined with books, and a sea chest and stool in the corner. The light from the window spotlighted a photograph case and book, lying on top of the pillow.

Trying to ignore the temptation to snoop, I scooped up the bundle of dirty clothes. My conscience scolded me as I turned back at the door and reached out to touch the case. With trembling fingers, I unfastened the case's latch and lifted the lid, unsure what I would find. Partly convinced it would only be a photograph of grandmother or grandfather, I caught my breath when I saw the image staring back at me: a beautiful young woman. I saw her dark hair, soft eyes, sweet expression, and expensive gown in the clear black and white portrait.

"Who are you?" I murmured. "And why does Uncle have your photograph?" It wasn't Mama, and it didn't look like Aunt Susannah. It certainly wasn't Grandmama. Their small photographs stood downstairs on the bookcase in the parlor. Hesitatingly, I shifted the laundry and picked up the case, turning it over to look for an inscription. Nothing, though the case did appear slightly water damaged. Then I noticed a small engraved plaque below the photograph. Straining my eyes, I read the inscription: M. Jamison.

"Susan dear," Mama called from below, "is this all the laundry?"

With shaky hands, I replaced the photograph, picked up the laundry, and darted out the door, closing it behind me. I felt guilty; I had been prying and looking at something which I hadn't been told I could see.

Wondering if I should confess to Mama or Uncle Richard presented a problem. If I told Mama, then I might be sharing something my uncle didn't want to talk about. If I told Uncle Richard, I didn't know what he would say. The morning moved slowly. I decided not to say anything right then. After all, the photograph had been sitting out, but I resolved not to look at things that weren't meant for me.

Still, I felt uncomfortable inside. However, the day was pleasant, and I sat on a blanket, minding Marian as Mama scrubbed, rinsed, and wrung the clothes. Today, Marian was determined to use her new crawling skills to get to the edge of the blanket and try to eat rocks. Time after time, I crawled after her and moved her back to the middle, sometimes prying a rock out of her chubby hand. Little clapping games and her blocks didn't interest her today, but those tempting rocks had captured her attention.

We often practiced school lessons while working on mindless tasks. Unsuccessfully, I tried to order my thoughts and respond when Mama tested me on my spelling words, but my mind could only remember "M. J-a-m-i-s-o-n."

"You will have to study that list of words again," Mama scolded mildly as she swished a shirt in the rinse water. "Are you thinking of writing? You can't be distracted like this or you won't make any progress in your schooling."

I shook my head. "No, I'm not thinking of poetry." I watched Paul, sitting in the shade and trying desperately to whistle "Yankee Doodle."

"Well, come help me hang the clothes on the line, and then you can go study the words. Jacob, leave Bonnie alone and come watch Marian so Susan can help me."

As I clipped the clean clothes on the clotheslines running between the lighthouse and the shed, I pondered the next question that came to mind. Who was M. Jamison? I couldn't think of anyone we knew with that name. Was the M for Margaret? A long kitchen towel waved in the breeze as I stretched up to clip it to the line. The thin, fluttering cloth reminded me of a bride's veil. Was Uncle Richard going to marry Margaret Jamison?

During the next days, I completed my chores, played with my siblings, studied my lessons, helped with the ironing and amusing Marian, and sewed my sampler. And I fought the impulse to sneak into my uncle's room and look at the photograph again. I tried to forget her and concentrate on my poetry. Yet I thought constantly about that beautiful lady and wanted to know who she was. Several times, I almost asked Uncle Richard. Each time I wasn't brave enough to say the words. If he had wanted us to know, he would have told us, I reasoned.

Chapter 10

"Susan Rose, do you know what today is?" Father said cheerily, a few days later as he came to the breakfast table.

"No, Father?" I questioned. I'd been so preoccupied thinking about Miss Jamison and weaving a new poem about a secret heiress who steals the heart of a wandering knight that I had lost track of the calendar dates.

"Does June second seem like a special day to you?" he replied with a mischievous smile.

"Oh, it's my birthday!" I exclaimed, surprised that I had forgotten. "I'm ten years old today." I wondered if Jane and Anna remembered my birthday and if they were thinking of me today.

"Happy birthday, happy birthday..." Jacob and Paul chanted. Marian squealed, sensing the excitement.

Mama came in, carrying a platter of pancakes which she placed on the table. "Happy day, my beautiful Susan," she said, giving me a kiss on the cheek and a hug. Uncle Richard announced his joyful wishes from his seat across the table.

The day passed with normal chores and schoolwork, but Mama promised we would eat supper early and have a special celebration before the light watches began. I looked forward to it with anticipation all day, wondering what we would do. For Paul's birthday last November, we had played hide-n-seek, and for Jacob's, Father had taught us charades. And with an excited, fluttery feeling in my stomach, I wondered what my birthday presents would be. Last year, Mama had let us girls walk into the nearby town and buy peppermint sticks, and then we'd played on the big swing at Anna's house until suppertime. Mama had surprised me with a cake, and the boys had picked flowers for me. Memories prompted loneliness, so I pushed them away, wrote some poetry, and looked forward to this evening's fun.

After supper – crab cakes, biscuits, carrots, and cookies – Father said it was time for birthday presents. I got to sit in the rocking chair.

"Close your eyes," Jacob ordered. "Hold out your hands." Something small and square was placed on my palms.

"Open!" Paul exclaimed. "We made it for you." It was a small wooden box decorated with little seashells.

"I like it, and it will be perfect to keep my hair ribbons in," I said, smiling. "Thank you, Jacob and Paul."

After I had admired the little box for a few minutes and heard about each shell, Uncle Richard said, "Alright, boys, my turn. Close your eyes, Susan."

Something slender and flat was placed in my hand, and I opened my eyes. "Oh, how pretty," I exclaimed, holding up a small, decorative hair comb delicately carved with a pattern of vines and flowers.

"Do you know what it's made of?" Uncle Richard asked, kneeling beside my chair.

"Whalebone," I guessed, remembering some of the carved pins Mama had. I ran my finger over the carving, marveling at its smoothness.

"Good girl," he smiled. "You were raised to be wise in the ways of the sea." With an offering gesture, he took the comb and slid it in place at the top of my braid. For once, I didn't think Uncle Richard was hiding. He seemed at ease and genuinely pleased to be celebrating with us. I smiled at him, and he smiled back.

Father told me to close my eyes again, and something large and paper wrapped was placed in my hands. Underneath the ribbon and old newspaper, I found a straw hat with cheery yellow ribbon gathered around the low crown and long yellow ties hanging below. "Oh, it's perfect," I sighed. "And just in time for summer too! Thank you."

"You're welcome," Mama answered, and Father smiled. "If it's a windy day, you can borrow one of my hatpins," Mama assured me.

"Now that we've had gifts, how are we going to celebrate?" Jacob wanted to know.

"Well, we have three-quarters of an hour before the light must be lit. How about...music and dancing?" Father suggested. Uncle Richard and Father sang lively, rousing songs, and Jacob, Paul, and I twirled and darted around the room.

"We must show these children how to dance, Harriet," Father announced, after watching our wild and silly attempts. He invited Mama to dance and hummed a quick waltz.

"Now a simple, faster dance," Father called, changing the tune.

Father spun Mama away from him, and she took Jacob's hands while Father bowed to me with mock formality. Calling the dance steps to me, we began. "Heel, toe, heel toe. Now we slide, slide, slide. Same thing back the other way. Clap!" There was a pattern to the clapping, and it made me giggle. Over and over, we danced the pattern, laughing and getting faster every time.

Finally, the rhythm was simply too fast, and Father collapsed dramatically in his rocking chair. Breathless, I plopped down on the floor, smiling and laughing.

Mama came and leaned over Father's chair. He grinned up at her. "Whew! I'm afraid I'm not as young as I used to be. Tired already."

Mama laughed, but I was disappointed. "I want to dance more, please."

"I'll dance with you, Susan," Uncle Richard said, "but your father will have to sing for our music."

Uncle Richard taught me the simple steps for a jig. Then Father sang a rollicking sea chantey, and we danced, arms crossed, facing each other until Uncle Richard declared he needed a break too.

"I didn't know you could dance," I panted as I sat down on the floor and looked up at my uncle. "I didn't know you carved whale bone either."

"So many surprises," he replied mysteriously.

The low fire crackled in the hearth, warding off the chilly damp. "You are more like yourself," Mama commented. "Like the brother I knew so many years ago. It's good." He nodded, looking relaxed.

I picked up the forgotten newspaper wrapping and smoothed it out. In the late light, words about the war caught my eye. Uncle Richard looked down over my shoulder. "May I see that?"

He took the paper and seemed to read a section. His expression changed from openness to frowning suspicion. His hands clenched around the edges of the paper; it crunched in his grasp.

Eyeing Uncle Richard, I inched away from him to where the boys were looking at the box they had made for me. "Tell me about that shell again?" I asked. "Where did you find it?" Paul described the exact location down by the boat dock. Then Jacob told how he had looked at shells in Father's book about animals and nature. He started to explain some of the things he and Father had read when Uncle Richard stamped his foot, startling us all.

"It's a lie. It's all a lie," he exclaimed, crushing the newspaper into a ball and launching it into the fireplace. As we stared at him, he sprang from the chair and hurried out of the room, calling, "Forgive me" in a broken voice.

Mama followed her brother. I knelt in front of the glowing coals. Headline words like "traitor" and "loyalty" darkened as a tongue of flame licked at the newspaper. I didn't know if it was this article which upset Uncle Richard, but clearly something in that paper about the war had hurt him. Above, the footsteps echoed, a door slammed. Crouched by the fire, I started crying.

Father shushed the boys' questions and sent them to check the goats' water. Silently, he placed Marian in her cradle box with a toy and went upstairs to tend the light. I couldn't tell if he was upset or didn't know what to say.

I reached up and loosened the hair comb. Holding it in one hand, I traced the designs with a finger. I wished I could turn back the clock to the happy moments and erase the more recent anger and retreat.

Mama came back, and she had been crying too. "I don't know why," Mama answered my unspoken question. "I'm sorry this happened, especially on your birthday."

"I thought he was getting happier. Then this."

Without resolution or answers, we waited in the darkening room. Mama held me tightly. "I wish..." Mama whispered into my hair, but she did not finish her thought aloud.

Father entered the room, saying, "Richard did take his assigned first watch." Then he noticed Mother's expression. "Harriet?"

"In the morning, I'll tell him," Mama said angrily calm.

"Wait. You'll tell him what?"

Mama released me, saying gently, "Go to your room, Susan." As I left, she answered Father, "He needs to go. I'll not have him disrupting my children with outbursts like this."

"He's unstable, Harriet. He needs to stay. If you send him away, you may never see him again. I am exercising my authority as head lighthouse keeper tonight. Richard Bates stays, and we do everything in our power to keep him here, though I will keep a closer eye on him and his work."

Their voices weren't loud, but they got quieter, and as I went upstairs, I couldn't hear the argument anymore. I didn't know if I wanted Uncle Richard to stay or go. I couldn't decide. His secret – whatever it was – seemed dangerous to himself and maybe to us.

Chapter 11

The next morning Uncle Richard shuffled to the breakfast table. "I want to apologize for my actions last evening. Even though I was angry, I shouldn't have responded that way. Forgive me?" We nodded. "Susan, I'm sorry for spoiling your celebration."

I wanted to tell him it was alright, but it wasn't. I wanted to ask what was wrong. I wanted Father to sit Uncle Richard in a chair and make him confess those lurking secrets. I wanted no more darkness and forbidden shadows. And I could not say all those things. "Forgive you," I murmured, glancing at Mama and noticing her set jaw.

She cornered Uncle Richard at the cistern later that morning. I couldn't hear what she said, but from her gestures, she expressed her frustration and pleaded for answers. He faced her with his arms crossed.

Later that morning when I playfully chased Mattie out from under my bed and clutched her in my arms to take her downstairs, I heard angry voices in the watchroom above.

"Samuel, I can't tell you," Uncle Richard said. "I'm no criminal, but some of my past actions could cause trouble for you. No one here knows. No one can find me here. I will not tell you."

"I could mention this to the inspector," Father threatened.

"You could," Uncle Richard shot back. "And there's a chance I would lose my position. Have I done anything that would cause you to question my integrity or loyalty on this job?" There was a pause. "Can you not trust me?" His voice quieted.

I squeezed Mattie so tightly that she meowed fretfully, and I let her go. I crossed my empty arms and sat down on the bed. Who was searching for him in the busy world?

"He has to stay," I said to the empty room. "We have to help him."

During the rest of the day, Uncle Richard avoided all of us. He decided not to come down to dinner and probably wouldn't have come to supper, except Mama insisted. Sitting across the table from me, he kept his eyes on his food. Uncomfortable silence created an awkward meal, and I pushed the food around on my plate.

"Perhaps I should walk to town tomorrow and see if we have any letters," Uncle Richard said, glancing at Father. "These June days are long enough that I could go there and back in plenty of time. Maybe even hitch a ride in a wagon so I don't have to walk all the way."

"Will you come back?" Mama asked, looking like she might cry.

"Of course. It's just…we might have quite a stack of correspondence waiting."

I knew it was about five miles to the nearest town, and sometimes we had walked along the path a little ways, just for fun. Father had said that path joined a main road which led to the inland community.

"That's fine," Father replied.

Mama spoke up, "Could you get a few grocery items for me? We're low on coffee, tea, and salt. I'll make a list. There are probably other items, and it still might be a few weeks before the inspector arrives with our regular supplies." Uncle Richard nodded. "Oh, and I should write to Mother and Susannah tonight. You could post the letters for us. Susan, would you like to write to your friends?"

I didn't know. Part of me wanted to write. Part of me wanted to ignore my friends. In a strange way, I reasoned that if I didn't write to them I wouldn't miss them as much. Mama looked at me expectantly, and I finally said, "Yes, I'll write."

That letter to Jane and Anna challenged me. I couldn't tell them I was lonely, but I didn't want the girls to think I didn't care about them. I told them about the garden boxes, my sampler, and the rug Mama and I had made for my room. When Mama read the letter, she praised my penmanship and complimented my writing style. Uncle Richard spent the evening hours before his light watch in his room, and I wondered if he wrote a letter to someone.

Later, lying awake in bed, I tossed and turned. I didn't trust Uncle Richard. He was running away from something. Us? His anger? Or the awakened memories from his past? I felt guilty for being judgmental. After all, I had my own secret that I wouldn't face.

I must have slept because a slight noise woke me in the early morning. Then I heard footsteps in the hallway. I ran to my door and poked my head out. "Uncle Richard," I whispered, startling him. "Will you come back?"

"Yes," he promised. "If I leave this lighthouse, I will resign. Not run away. Neglecting duty is something I've never done." Despite the darkened hallway, I could see enough of his expression to understand he meant every word. This was the way a captain would speak. The tone of a man who refused to compromise.

"See you tonight then," I answered. "Have a good trip."

"Aye, aye, miss," he replied, heading down the stairs.

Throughout the day from Father's gruff attitude and Mama's watchful glances toward the inland path, I knew they questioned if Uncle Richard would come back. The boys asked. Marian scanned the room and looked every time someone came in the door as though she missed her uncle who was still scared of her. I believed my uncle, but fear tightened inside me.

We did our chores, and later, when finished with our schoolwork, Mama let us play outside. We didn't feel like playing, so we sat by the garden boxes, talking. The boys discussed Uncle Richard's new job, firmly convinced he wasn't coming back.

"He'll be back," I said again and again.

When Paul scampered off to pet the goats, Jacob turned to me and said solemnly, "I have a secret. You can't tell anyone." He straightened his shirt and leaned close. "I want to be a naturalist when I grow up. Father said that's a person who studies animals."

"Really?"

"Yes. When Paul and I were collecting the shells to make your birthday box, I asked Father lots of questions. So many questions that he had to get out his big book about different kinds of animals, and one afternoon, we read the whole section about shellfish. I didn't understand all of it, but it was really interesting. I want to study and draw animals when I grow up. That's my big secret."

"Your big secret?" It seemed so grand it didn't need to be a secret. "I think it's a good goal." I tried to imagine what we'd all do when we grew up, but I couldn't quite imagine what would happen in the next hour – let alone events that were years away.

The sun had started its slow descent toward the inland horizon. What if my uncle had lied? I just couldn't believe that – not this time. His tone and words this morning had convinced me. But he had gone to the world outside our lighthouse, a world where someone might be looking for him. What if he was captured or arrested and didn't come back?

Then we'd all think he was a liar, when really… What was the truth? We didn't even know that.

"Uncle Richard's coming!" Paul shouted, running around the shed's corner and interrupting my worried thoughts.

I turned and saw him coming toward us. Coming home? Did he think of the lighthouse as a home and us as close family? He looked tired, I thought, carrying that sack of groceries.

The boys ran to meet him, and I followed. When he saw us, he waved his arm crazily, making us laugh, making me hope the incidents and mistrust could be forgotten.

As the boys ran back to the lighthouse to tell Mama about Uncle Richard's return, I walked with him. "You came back."

"Did you think I wouldn't? What would you do without someone to read your poetic scribblings to?" His cheerful words sounded forced. Glancing up, I noticed his sad expression and hunched shoulders. When he saw I was watching, he shrugged, saying with a brittle smile, "Long walk…and I did linger in town. But I am glad to be back."

"Is everything alright now?" I asked, concerned. "Did we get a bad letter or something?"

"No, everything's fine." His words were reassuring, but his tone was hollow. I did not believe him.

"Did you post my letter to the girls?"

"Of course. I wouldn't forget something so important," he teased gently.

By the time we reached the house, Uncle Richard had completely concealed that weary, sorrowful expression. Mama waited for him at the door with a welcoming smile and hug while Marian reached her chubby arms toward him and giggled.

That evening after an early supper Mama read aloud the letters from Grandmama and Aunt Susannah, and then Father opened the current newspaper and began summarizing the reports from the nation to us. Glancing around, it seemed as though the last days had only been an unhappy dream. Mama and Father were willing to forget if they could. In the time before the first evening watch, Uncle Richard sat a little farther away than usual as we heard the news, but that was his choice.

Father read about debates on a newly purchased territory of the United States in the far northwest; the paper called it Alaska and said it was just a frozen wasteland. He started to read aloud about Indian fighting on the western plains but then changed to a different column which discussed President Andrew Johnson's arguments with Congress over Reconstruction – how to rebuild the South after the war. I thought the Indians would've been more frightfully exciting than the release of the former Confederate president and increasing tension between the President Johnson and Congress.

Father explained, "This is a difficult situation. Johnson doesn't want to do things Congress's way. And many congressmen aren't please."

"But the Confederates were bad, weren't they? Shouldn't they be punished? They were disloyal." I remembered all those old newspaper accounts and felt sure Father would agree with my opinion.

"Disloyal is a big word," Father said. "Both sides claimed they were loyal to original American ideas in the Constitution."

"And those who didn't really want the war were caught in the middle," Uncle Richard added, getting up to go light the lamps and begin the watch.

I decided the big words and ideas were confusing. Besides, the war and its effects didn't concern me beyond my own curiosity to read the old newspapers. Father hadn't fought. Uncle Richard said he wasn't a soldier. Why did I need to care now?

Chapter 12

B ang! I sat up in bed, startled at the gunshot.

"Happy Fourth of July!" Father shouted from outside.

I laughed and shook my head as I climbed out of bed. Drawing aside the curtains, I leaned out the open window, calling, "You did it again, Father." He stood below, wearing his work clothes: plaid shirt, brown trousers, and suspenders.

"Did what, Susan Rose?" he asked innocently.

"Scared us on Fourth of July!"

He grinned, good-naturedly brandishing the pistol. "I've been shooting blank rounds every year you can remember. It's to remind us of the war to win our independence. Get dressed and make your bed quickly. I have a surprise for later on."

"More gunshots? Firecrackers?" I guessed. Jane, Anna, and I had thought firecrackers were the best, and our fathers had made quite a show of them down the by the lake last year.

"Get ready and you'll find out," he replied.

Jiggling and bouncing on the hard wood benches around the breakfast table, the boys tried to guess what the surprise would be. Marian squealed and pounded her spoon on the table until Mama corrected her. Uncle Richard announced he didn't know either, and Mama said it wasn't her secret to tell. I don't think we ever did our chores so quickly.

Finally, with morning work finished, we all gathered outside in the brilliant sunlight. I spun around in my new pink calico dress which Mama had finished a couple weeks earlier. Father had turned a packing box upside down, climbed on it, and said he was going to make a grand speech. In the hushed and eager expectation, we heard the faint crunching of wagon wheels on rock. Surprised, I turned and saw a wagon coming toward the lighthouse.

"Visitors," Mama said, smiling. "Not uncommon on a holiday."

Father jumped off the box with an embarrassed glance. "To be continued," he announced, tucking his speech paper back in his pocket.

I frowned, torn between the excitement of seeing new folks and disliking strangers tramping through our home. It was different than inviting friends to visit. At our old lighthouse, strangers came nearly every Saturday afternoon in the summer and always on Fourth of July. They had liked to poke into our rooms, and once someone stole all my hair ribbons. It was one of the trials and pleasures of living in a lighthouse. As Mama frequently reminded us, a lighthouse was government property, so our house really belonged to all the American people, not just to us. If someone wanted to come to the lighthouse, they must be made welcome.

Fortunately, our visitors today seemed like a pleasant family – Mr. and Mrs. Crawford, their four older children, and grandmother. Mrs. Crawford had brought a lovely bouquet of flowers for Mama and a lattice-topped pie. As head lightkeeper, Father welcomed them and offered to give them a tour of the lighthouse.

The boys and I sat quietly in the entry hall, listening to the visitors' marveling exclamations about the views of the beauty from the windows and lantern as they came downstairs again.

"And do you like living here, Miss Arnold?" Mrs. Crawford asked me sweetly as she descended the last steps. "It must be very peaceful."

I stood and responded politely, "I like being a lightkeeper's daughter. But it is a lot of work to keep the house nice and neat, and it's really not peaceful when it storms." I willed myself not to think about the loneliness.

"No, I should imagine not," she replied, smiling.

"But I like living close to the water. It has inspired some of the epic poetry I'm writing." I smiled, thinking of the fanciful legends I had woven.

"Really?" Mrs. Crawford answered, a sour look crossing her face. "Your mother allows you to write frivolously?" She snapped open her fan with a superior look at her daughters.

I sensed that I'd said something Mrs. Crawford didn't like but thought it was best to respond honestly now. "Yes, ma'am. She says it's fine as long as my chores and schoolwork are finished. She says it's good for me to be creative."

"Well, I don't approve of girls and women writing anything except letters. They will end up bold spinsters, writing for money in publications." The feathers on Mrs. Crawford's bonnet fluttered as she shook her head. "As for creativity, there is music and artwork which society deems appropriate for ladies. Most of all, they should spend their time taking care of their house and children. I am sending my girls to a finishing school, but they know very well that their place in the world is the home…and nowhere else."

"I don't have a house of my own or children," I responded innocently. She only frowned and walked out the door. "And until I do, I'll help Mama…and write," I whispered, pushing away the longing for true friends who would have come to our lighthouse on the lake for Fourth of July.

I felt like I'd been wrapped in a cold, wet blanket of harsh disappointment. Was writing contrary to being a lady? But Mama would never let me do something wrong. Someone laid a firm, kind hand on my shoulder. I looked up. It was Uncle Richard. "Never mind, Susan," he whispered, leaning down. "I'm told that the great artists and writers are not always appreciated when they are just beginning."

"Do you really like my poetry? I want to know the truth."

"Sometimes your dramatics are amusing and far overdone, but you seem to have a good grasp of how to rhyme."

We walked outside together, seeking to get away from the visitors. "Uncle Richard, what was the worst thing anyone ever said to you?"

"Something my niece should never hear."

"No, I didn't mean bad words. But did someone say something that hurt?"

"Her words hurt you?" he asked. When I nodded, he sighed, crossed his arms, and looked out at the sea. "Take care of her."

"What?" I looked up at him.

"Those were the words. 'Take care of her.'" He sighed again. "It's the words of a captain to his officer as he turns over the ship for a watch or a day in port. It's the instruction of any man relinquishing something precious. I always took it so seriously." He kicked at a loose rock. "Until one day. I couldn't. I lost her."

"The ship on the lake?" I questioned.

"That too. That too." Uncle Richard shook his head.

"So you're the assistant keeper," bellowed Mr. Crawford, coming up behind us and clapping Uncle Richard on the shoulder. Both of us jumped in startled surprise. "What did you say your name was?"

"I don't know that I had..." Uncle Richard muttered, then responded properly. "Bates. Richard Bates."

"Pleased to meet you. Say, you're not any relation to that fellow in the war, are you?"

"Oh, you mean that colonel? No. No, relation."

"I was meaning the..."

"My dear," Mrs. Crawford called shrilly, "We want to have a picnic down below. There's a sandy spot near the boat dock, the keeper says."

"Well, some other time then. If you are that fellow, I can't imagine what you're doing in a place like this," Mr. Crawford said, turning and walking back to the wagon.

I looked up at my uncle. "I know, I know. You want to know. There was some officer during the war with my name, and people want to know if I'm that fellow. I'm not. I wasn't a military officer." He scuffed his boot in annoyance.

That didn't answer Mr. Crawford's unfinished sentence, but I knew it was the only answer I'd get. Accepting this unwillingly, I followed my uncle back to the lighthouse and found my brothers.

The Crawfords had brought food baskets and spread their picnic blanket on the little strip of sandy beach not far from the dock. The boys and I took turns peering over the rocks until Mama called us away. Their outing seemed pleasant, but at the end, Mrs. Crawford marched up the path, loudly complaining about the wind while Mr. Crawford and the others puffed along behind, carrying the baskets and blanket.

They said good-bye, and Father politely thanked them for visiting. Uncle Richard and I breathed a sigh of relief when the wagon disappeared along the path into the trees.

Jacob bounced up and down. "Now, Father, please, can we finish whatever you were going to say?"

"Ah, yes. Gather everyone," Father said, carrying his box back to its original place.

When we were all assembled, Father climbed on the platform, pulled out the sheet of paper and, looking very solemn, started his Fourth of July speech. He had the paper unfolded and was just ready to begin when Paul hollered, "The goats are in the garden."

Sure enough, the goats were at the garden boxes, feasting on our little plants. "Come on boys," I called, starting to run, "we have to get them out of the garden. They're eating... Oh, no! Father...Uncle Richard...Run!" It was hard to run and shout clear sentences.

"Naughty, naughty goats!" Paul called, rushing ahead while the men stopped to get some ropes.

"How are we going to get them?" Jacob asked, stopping and tousling his hair.

"We'll just lead them back," I called, panting.

That was easier said than done. As we ran, Bonnie looked at us and cocked her head, but Patches kept munching contentedly. Just when we got close enough to grab their collars, the goats darted away, circled the garden, and stopped for a bite as we tried to catch up.

"Go that way. I'll go this way," Jacob shouted. "Then we'll trap them." It was a good idea, except Patches playfully butted Paul while Bonnie evaded my grasp, and I tumbled on the ground.

"We'll never catch them," I wailed in frustration and pain, rubbing my hands and knees to stop the stinging in the new scrapes.

Father came and authoritatively fastened his rope to Patches's collar, pulling her away from the tempting feast. Uncle Richard scooped up Bonnie and headed for the stable shed. Father looked critically around the shed as we refastened the gate. "This won't do," he said. "The shed really isn't big enough for them, and they don't get much room to walk around even when we tie them to the outside door. We don't have enough lumber for an outdoor pen. Maybe we could rig some sort of stake to tie them outside. That's a good project for tomorrow."

"Tomorrow's tomorrow," Jacob shouted, jumping up and down in the doorway, "and we still haven't seen the Fourth of July surprise."

For the third time that day, Father climbed on his wooden box while we stood waiting. He pulled out his speechifying paper and began to read, "Dearly beloved family, we are gathered here today in the sight of God…"

Mama tried to stifle her laughter, and Father gave her a playful glare. "Madam, I am making a speech."

"Yes, dear," she replied, "but it sounds like the beginning of a wedding ceremony."

Father smirked. "But you interrupted. We are celebrating Fourth of July, not a wedding. Now, let me begin again."

He tugged at his coat lapel and started, "Dearly beloved family, we are gathered again here today in the sight of God to give thanks for this beautiful land He has made and blessed. We are privileged with the task of guarding a portion of the coastline and tending to the beautiful light," he motioned grandly to the lighthouse, "which produces a prodigious amount of smoke and soot and keeps us awake at all hours of the night." Uncle Richard chuckled at Father's solemn statement. Father grinned back at him, then resumed his stern look.

"And yet it is a great privilege to know that our light keeps passing ships from running aground on these wicked rocks. Since we are tasked with so great a mission by the great government of the United States of America, I think it only right and proper that we should fly the flag of our country at our lighthouse. It will declare our national loyalty and love of country. Therefore, I have cobbled together a flagpole, which – if Mr. Richard Bates will help me – we will erect there," he pointed to a prepared location, "and raise the flag of our country, and it will be the duty of the children of the lighthouse to raise and lower the flag each day. Thank you fellow citizens, countrymen, and family for your attention to my short speech."

Jacob, Paul, and I cheered with excitement. We were going to have a real flagpole and a flag!

It didn't take Father and Uncle Richard very long to raise and secure the flagpole. A simple pulley system raised and lowered hooks to attach the flag. "Susan Rose, will you raise the flag for the first time at Herdman Point?" Father asked.

Nodding proudly, I took the sewn flag Mama handed me which she had been hiding in a basket. "I made it in the evenings after you went to bed," she said when I asked her.

Carefully, I clipped the flag onto the hooks and pulled the rope. The rising flag fluttered grandly as I raised it to the top of the pole. Father showed me how to tie it in place. Squinting into the bright sunlight, I watched the Stars and Stripes flying in the breeze, confidently proclaiming the unity and liberty in our country.

"Isn't it glorious?" I asked Uncle Richard, who stood near me. "That beautiful flag? I wonder if I could write poetry about it."

"It is nice," he replied simply, and I looked at him, surprised at his lack of enthusiasm. "So much has been given so that flag can fly."

"You mean by George Washington's patriots?" I asked.

"Certainly. And in the recent war, things were lost which can never be replaced."

Searching for a clue for my uncle's sadness, I replied, "Did someone you know die in a battle?"

"No. But they were a casualty of war. They were killed because of the war." He turned abruptly and walked away.

I looked back at the flag, staring at it as if it could give up secrets.

Chapter 13

As the July days passed, we children became skilled at raising and lowering the flag and took turns each day. Once Jacob forgot to bring in the flag at night, and Father explained to us the importance of treating the flag with respect. Military units traditionally raised the flag in the morning and lowered it at night, and we would do the same at our lighthouse.

"I won't let it happen again," Jacob promised. He sighed wistfully, "I wish someone would come visit so we could show them our new flag."

"We may have a visitor sooner than you think. Inspector Milton will be coming," Father said.

"Will he like the flag?" Paul wondered.

More importantly, I thought, will he be pleased with our lightkeeping? Though we all did our work consistently and knew we didn't need to be afraid of dismissal, it was still worrisome to know the inspector was coming soon.

"I'm sure he will," Father reassured. "Children, I want you to make sure you keep your toys and books put away neatly when you are not using them and be ready to help your mama with any extra chores."

Since Mama was such a good housekeeper, there wasn't too much extra work to accomplish, but there was always nervous expectation before the inspector's arrival. That afternoon Mama ironed our best clothes and hung them in our rooms, ready to be put on as soon as the inspector's ship was spotted. I pressed the best plaid tablecloth and napkins and laid them aside, ready to be put on the table as soon as we saw the inspector coming.

Four days passed. Every time I heard Father or Uncle Richard come in, I expected them to say it was time to get ready. All of us lived in anxious anticipation of the moment when the flurry of last minute preparations must happen. I remembered that odd confrontation between Inspector Milton and Uncle Richard and wondered how both of them would interact this time.

One morning we sat at the table, working on our lessons. Mattie crouched on my lap, licking my hand when I stopped stroking her fur to turn a page in my history book. The boys frowned at each other; Jacob had taken the longer piece of chalk that Paul wanted. I yawned. World history – especially the scanty details about Ancient Greece

– was not very interesting, even if Homer did write truly epic poetry.

The back door slammed, and Father called, "Inspector's coming. I spotted his boat."

Jacob sprang up and started stacking the schoolbooks. "Hurry, Paul, we have to get ready," he ordered our younger brother who was still tracing alphabet letters on the slate. In his haste, Jacob knocked Mama's cup of tea off the table; the liquid splattered, and the china cup shattered.

"Oh, dear," Mama exclaimed, coming into the room and seeing the mess. "Children, put away your books and go put on your nice clothes. Take your time, and don't make messes in your haste. We have at least an hour before he actually arrives."

I took Marian upstairs and put on the pretty little dress Mama had prepared for her. I set her on my bed and tied a little handkerchief doll so she could play. Marian swung and tossed the doll while I tried to get myself ready. With nervous fingers, I fastened the bone buttons on the bodice of my pink calico dress and smoothed the trim on the skirt and sleeves. The skirt flared prettily over my little hoopskirt and swished elegantly as I turned to pick up Marian and go downstairs.

We children sat lined-up on a bench in the main room, trying not to fidget as we waited for the inspector to come. The remains of the broken tea cup were already swept away, and as Mama pulled her freshly baked bread from the oven, she reminded us not to talk unless spoken to and to be polite.

In the parlor, Father straightened the pens on the desk one last time and opened the record books.

The clock ticked. Upstairs, Uncle Richard thumped hastily around his room. Marian tried to mess up my hair. The boys attempted to play cat's cradle, stopping and thrusting the string into Jacob's pocket every time they heard a strange noise. Waiting was never fun. I'll have to remember this feeling of nervous anticipation, I thought. It is the feeling a princess should have as she waits in the castle, fearing to hear the fate of her beloved warrior.

"He's coming ashore in the little boat now," Father said from the entry hall. Then his voice rose a notch, and he spoken urgently, "Boys, the goats are out and off their tether lines. Please go get them and put them in the shed."

"See, you didn't tie the knot right," Paul scolded as he ran after Jacob. They darted through the kitchen and toward the back door, Mama calling a warning not to get dirty as she rushed upstairs to pin on her fine brooch. I stayed in the main room and, through the window, saw them catch Patches without any trouble, but Bonnie was in a frisky mood, refusing to come or follow her mother. Sensibly, they took Patches toward the shed.

Inspector Milton appeared, striding up the path toward the lighthouse. I saw the boys peek out of the shed and guessed they would wait there until he came inside the house. Relieved, I supposed the adventure was over.

Then a drafty breeze from the kitchen made me realize the back door hadn't been latched all the way and must have blown open. As I went to close it, I found Bonnie staring at me from the doorway. She scampered into the kitchen and danced into the main room, staying just out of my reach. After seating Marian safely on the floor, I went after Bonnie, thankful that the door from the main room into the entryway was closed.

I heard the front door open, and Father and the inspector came inside. Bonnie's hoofs clattered as she taunted me with little jumps and frolics. In desperation, I cornered her, finally got hold of her collar, and tugged the wayward kid toward the door, but she didn't want to go. Franticly fearing what might happen if the inspector saw a goat in the house, I managed to lift Bonnie off the ground and staggered through the kitchen with the squirming animal, breathing a sigh as we got outside. I decided to tie her to the nearby picket stake Father had built for the goats.

"Naughty, naughty," I whispered, straightening my sleeves. I felt something tugging on the back of my dress. Surprised, I saw Bonnie nibbling on my skirt. I pushed her away and moved from her reach. Thankfully, there was only a wet spot near the hem, no holes. Not wanting to risk more disaster, I fled to the house and scooped Marian into my arms, just as Mama corralled the boys in through the entryway. Silently, we sat down on a bench near the table and waited. We could hear the men talking in the parlor with long breaks in the conversation when Inspector Milton was probably reading the record books.

Next, the men went outside, and we saw them pass the windows of the main room, looking at the structure, the newly painted trim, shutters, and frames, and the condition of the building. "The inspector looks pleased, don't you think?" I whispered to Mama.

"He should be. Your father and uncle have done well." She knit quickly as though she couldn't sit still unless her hands were busy.

We heard them come inside and go upstairs. "I might have left my jumping jack man on my bed," Paul said, his lower lip starting to quiver. "Will that make Inspector mad?"

"I don't think so," Mama answered. "Don't cry, Paul. If you had toys all over the house and we hadn't swept in a week, that would be bad. But one toy not put away will probably be alright." She glanced at me. "Marian looks like she is almost asleep. Could you put her in her cradle box in the corner?"

I laid my sister in her little bed and covered her with a light blanket, then came back and sat down, trying not to be too nervous. Beside me, Jacob fidgeted, weaving his fingers together and them exploding them apart. He stopped when he heard the men coming back.

The door opened, and they entered. "Well done, gentlemen," the inspector announced, shaking Father's hand. "Everything appears to be in good order in the books. The exterior and interior are in excellent condition. I commend you for keeping a good lighthouse. This is a fine example of lighthouse keeping. I especially like the new flag and flagpole. Very nice."

The boys and I grinned. He had noticed!

Outside, Bonnie bleated impatiently. I watched the inspector, hoping he wouldn't think anything bad about our noisy little goat. Thankfully, he didn't seem to hear Bonnie.

The inspector turned and shook Uncle Richard's hand. He knit his brow and leaned closer to my uncle, asking, "Were you ever shipwrecked?"

Uncle Richard wiped his hands on his trousers, swallowed, and replied, "Yes, sir."

"Where?" the inspector inquired, frowning and crossing his arms.

"Lake Michigan."

Inspector Milton raised his bushy eyebrows. "Not the Carolina coast? What did you do during the late war?"

"I was in Europe, working in a chandlery store."

That alerted me like a ship's alarm bell. Uncle Richard had told us he had been shipwrecked when returning to America from his time in Europe. Why did he only mention the lost ship on the Great Lake?

"Are you sure we haven't crossed paths before?" the inspector asked, looking my uncle in the eye.

"I don't know, sir," Uncle Richard replied with honest sincerity in his tone. "I'm not sure there's anything about your features that would specially distinguish you from other men with brown beards and blue eyes, if we only met briefly."

Father and Mama looked questioningly at each other. The boys and I were quiet, puzzled.

"Perhaps it is just my imagination," Inspector Milton shrugged, turning away. He started toward the door, then stopped. "You look remarkably like a man I once saw on a beach after a shipwreck. You look like a man I took prisoner in the war and who later escaped me. But perhaps it is just my imagination," he repeated, turning back to Uncle Richard as if hoping to catch an expression on his face.

Uncle Richard's hands tightened into fists, but the inspector did not notice. "Perhaps so," Uncle Richard said evenly.

"Loyalty is important in the lighthouse service," Inspector Milton declared emphatically. "Anyone not loyal to the United States has no business working in our lighthouses. And anyone who has borne arms against the Federal Government should not be hired by the Lighthouse Board."

"Is that a new regulation?" Father asked, looking confused.

"No, but it is my belief and what will be upheld in my district. My son was killed in the war. A man who wore gray and who could've killed my son should not be allowed to save lives." He looked at my uncle, but he met his gaze and didn't look away.

Squaring his jaw, Uncle Richard said firmly, emphasizing each word, "I did not wear gray."

The inspector turned abruptly and said to Father, "You – I'm sure – agree that loyalty is important. I speak generally and not specifically," he glanced at Uncle Richard, "when I say that you would never allow a traitor to the United States to keep a lighthouse."

"I do not doubt Mr. Bates's dedication to his duties," Father responded. "Yes, a lightkeeper must be loyal. His family too. Hard work keeps the light burning."

"Very well, very well. Come down to the dock. I have your food supplies and a letter or two to deliver to you. We'll do that and then maybe have a bite of food?"

"Of course," Mama said with a smile. He marched out the door.

Father put his hand on Uncle Richard's shoulder and said quietly, "Don't worry. Trust has to be earned. Loyalty can't be bought. Soon, he will respect your abilities and stop this questioning." Uncle Richard shrugged away Father's hand and headed for the door.

I sat down in the rocking chair. Had Uncle Richard told Father his secret? I didn't think so. But Father had defended him, making sure he would stay here with us. Father hadn't said a word about Uncle Richard's unknown past, even though we all knew he had something hidden.

Uncle Richard and the war. I wondered why he hadn't volunteered to save the Union and fight in President Lincoln's army. Yes, I knew he said he was in Scotland, but why hadn't he come back? How did he lose someone important because of the war if he wasn't in it? As the months passed, this war and its effects seemed closer and closer in the hidden shadows. Were the colors of those shadows blue and gray?

Mama called me to come help in the kitchen, and I didn't have more time to wonder. It took several hours for the men to move the barrels and boxes of supplies and stow them in the storage room and shed. The work was interrupted by dinner; the boys and I were almost too nervous to eat, but we were astonished at the amount of food Inspector Milton forked into his mouth.

The sun slid toward the land's horizon as the boys and I stood on the rocks and waved good-bye to the inspector's boat as it headed down the coast. The boys went to feed the goats, and after drawing a bucket of fresh water, I returned to the house. Uncle Richard sat on the back step, staring at nothing. His hands shook.

Frightened, I called Mama. "Richard, what's wrong?" she asked, kneeling in front of him and holding his hands.

"The past is never escapable," he said. "What one is suspected of is never gone. Even you, Harriet, are suspicious." He stood up, pulling away from her gentle grasp. "I tell you. I did nothing wrong. I sold ropes, navigation tools, maps, and such in a chandlery store. I tried to do what was right and was punished, cursed – I don't know what!" Uncle Richard opened the door and looked back at us, saying bitterly, "Loyalty... they – you – question that?"

Chapter 14

One afternoon as the late August sun shone through the windows and fluttering curtains, I lounged in the big rocking chair, my legs stuck over the arm. I balanced my school books and tried to focus on my studies. I wished I could go wading in the lake shallows, have a water fight with Jane and Anna, or playfully dunk my brothers. I longed to finish school and escape all these thoughts to work on my next poem. My latest imaginary world involved a fearsome sea monster who tricked sailors to a watery grave…not exactly cheerful, but I had started tiring of fairy tales with perfect endings.

Uncle Richard stumbled into the room and sat wearily in a chair by the empty hearth. He had been taking his regular afternoon nap but seemed disoriented.

"Are you well, Richard?" Mama asked, holding up her hand for Jacob to pause in his simple arithmetic tables.

He shivered, sighed, and shook his head. "I'm afraid it's my old enemy come back to trouble me."

"What enemy?" Paul asked, squeaking his slate chalk to a sudden stop.

"A sickness. But you can't get it, so you needn't worry. The doctors call it intermittent fever. Others call it chills and fever," he answered Mama's questioning look. "I got a bad case when I stopped at a port in the West Indies. It left me so weak that it took months to recover. The disease flares up every now and then." He leaned his head in his hands. "The headaches are the worst for me," he complained softly. "And it's not called fever and chills for no reason."

Mama raised her eyebrows. "Richard, why didn't you tell me before? We could've prepared by having better medicines on hand."

"I'll take your watches," Father said from the open parlor door. "You go to bed and rest until you're better."

"I'm sure I'll be alright," Uncle Richard protested, straightening.

"No. As head lightkeeper, I'm ordering you to rest. If you were to fall asleep or become very ill at your post, lives could be endangered."

"Thank you. I'm sorry. If it's alright, then, I'll go to bed." Uncle Richard sighed resignedly and retreated upstairs.

"Samuel, did he ever mention a trip to the West Indies to you?" Mama asked Father.

Father shook his head. "Intermittent fever is bad, though."

"I know," Mama answered softly.

That was the beginning of some very long days. Uncle Richard lay in his bed, too sick and tired to get up. Mama worried about his fever and kept trying different herbal teas while Father did double work around the lighthouse and stayed awake in the watchroom through all the hours of those summer nights.

I looked after the younger children with no time to think or write. "Jacob, hush," I snapped on the fourth day as he flapped around the room, clucking like a chicken. It rained outside – a summer storm with refreshing rain – but it meant we couldn't go outside to play. Paul lay down on one side of the main room and rolled to the other end; giggling, he caught Mattie by the tail and dragged her. Her frantic yowling added to the noise. Marian cackled at the boys' antics and pounded the wooden block in her fist on the floor. Putting my hands on my head, I despaired of ever keeping the house quiet. I picked up Marian.

"Boys, please!" I begged. "Uncle cannot rest with all the noise you are making. Paul, get up off the floor."

"But what can we do?" they whined together. "You wouldn't let us play hide-n-seek yesterday. Mama has been upstairs most of the last few days taking care of Uncle Richard."

I was tired. Too tired to write, but I was frustrated that I didn't have time since I had to watch my siblings every waking moment. "We could see who can stay quiet longest."

"Bor...ing," they groaned, dragging out the word.

"Let's shoot marbles. Do you think we could do that quietly?"

"Yes! Marbles." They crept upstairs to get their box.

I managed to calm Marian and laid her down for a nap in her cradle box. Then we sat on the large braided rug, laid out a scrap of yarn to form a circle, and put a dozen marbles inside the circle. Taking turns, we shot marbles at the ones in the circle, trying to knock them out.

A while later, Mama came into the room. "Thank you for quieting down," she said, looking weary and worried. She went into the kitchen to begin preparing supper.

"How is Uncle Richard?" I asked, leaving the game and following her.

"Not better. His fever is higher. He's not comfortable and keeps tossing and turning. This afternoon he started talking wildly." She wrung her hands on a towel. "If there was a doctor near, I would send for him."

The only doctor in the area was five miles away, and Uncle Richard must be very sick if Mama thought he needed a doctor. As long as I could remember, Mama usually had all the answers for little injuries and illnesses in her green book called *Family Nurse*. "You should go back to him, Mama," I whispered, hugging her so she couldn't see that I was about to cry. "We can eat bread and jam for one evening."

"Brave Susan," Mama murmured and held me tighter. "You are doing a fine job looking after the little ones. Thank you. You are becoming quite a capable young lady." She took a basin from the shelf, filled it from the water bucket, and went upstairs again.

Then I cried. Mama wanted to send for a doctor? That echoed in my mind. Was my uncle going to die? I prayed, dried my tears, and started setting the table for supper. I couldn't do anything for Uncle Richard right now, but chores and lighthouse duties had to go on. Outside, the rain stopped and the sky cleared.

Before sunset that evening, Father alternated his time between Uncle Richard's room and reading to us downstairs. Mama did not join us. "Bedtime," Father said, coming into the main room and picking up Marian to carry her to my room for tonight. We didn't necessarily have to go to sleep immediately, but with Father tending the light and Mama taking care of Uncle Richard, Father settled us in our rooms before his watch began.

Closing the bedroom door, I heard Father pause at Uncle Richard's door, say something to Mama, and then his slow, weary tread went up the stairs to the watchroom. I slipped on my nightgown and drew back the curtains from the open window. In bed, I couldn't close my eyes. The fears I had calmed earlier returned as dusk settled. Finally, I got up and stole out of my room, moving toward the dull lamp light and open door of my uncle's room.

Mama sat in a chair near her brother's bed. Leaning forward, she wrung out a cloth in a basin of water and wiped his forehead, then tried to still his restless twisting, speaking comfortingly. Uncle Richard tossed side to side on the pillow, and he muttered frantically, occasionally reaching out as if looking for something or someone. He did not seem to know Mama.

"Margaret, Margaret, I'm sorry, I'm sorry," he called repeatedly.

Mama turned and saw me. "Go to bed, Susan." She looked exhausted in the dim light from the oil lamp.

"I can't sleep," I admitted.

"You're afraid of what might happen?" she whispered, holding out her arms. "So am I. But we have to trust God." Mama held me close, and I felt her tears fall on my face. "I am afraid I wasn't as supportive as I should've been. That I secretly resented him for hiding his own secrets."

"Mama?" I couldn't believe her.

"I'm not perfect, Susan. Everyone has struggles."

"But you don't mind living in this lonely lighthouse away from our friends." Unlike me, I added inwardly.

"I should've been kinder, not as direct in my questions to him at the beginning. I was upset because he is not the brother I once knew, and I felt I had been unfair to my family. I should've been gentler and less worried about myself."

"Margaret...no," Uncle Richard moaned, trying to sit up and falling back again.

"Who is Margaret, Mama?" I asked. Did she know anything about the woman I had seen in the photograph? Should I tell her?

"I don't know. She was or is important to him, and I think something happened to her. At times, he says, 'It's my fault.' "

"Do you think he will get better?"

"God willing. He's very sick. Pray for him. I'm afraid we don't have the most effective medicines for this fever, but I keep trying with what we do have." She smoothed back my hair. "Would you do something for me? I know your father left some coffee to keep warm at the back of the stove. Could you take him a cup? He's not used to staying awake all night anymore."

A few moments later, I glided up the steep stairs to the watchroom, careful not to spill the hot drink in my hand. Father was surprised to see me, and I explained. I sat on the top stair for a while, watching the flashes of light out the window. After finishing his coffee, Father went up to the lantern to check the oil in the lamps. Below, Mama called urgently, "Richard, Richard." I ran down to the room.

Uncle Richard lay very quiet, not moving or muttering. His eyes were half-open, but he did not seem to see anything – it frightened me. Between Mama's quick words, I could hear him breathing. He did not rouse when she spoke to him.

"Is he asleep with his eyes open?" I whispered.

"No, if he would sleep that would be good. I cannot tell if the fever will break or if he will slip away now." She wiped her eyes. "He seems to be continually waiting or watching for something. Did he ever tell you or the boys anything?"

"No, Mama," I replied. I started crying. I didn't want my uncle to die. Mama tried to send me away, and I sniffled back my tears. "Do you think he can hear us?"

"I don't know," Mama admitted.

I went to the low bed and knelt down. I wanted to speak, but when I opened my mouth, I couldn't and hid my sobs in the mattress. I hadn't realized before that night how much I cared about my uncle. That he was truly part of our family, even with his secrets. What would we do without him? I couldn't imagine life at this lighthouse without him. Selfishly, I didn't want more happy memories to become painful. "Go to bed. It will be alright," Mama said, trying to lift me up.

I had to speak. What if I was the only one who knew? I didn't wipe away the tears, and I couldn't stop my voice from breaking, but I looked at him and knew I had to say it. "Uncle Richard, please live. We love you. And Margaret forgives you. Is she your beautiful dreamer?" I looked up at Mama. "That's his favorite song he said. Do you think it would help?" I couldn't sing, but I whispered the words I'd heard him serenade so many times.

He turned and muttered incoherently again, asking about the weather, fearing a storm, cursing somebody called "Yankee." Mama sent me away, and I crept back into my room, curled up on my bed, and cried.

I wanted to help my uncle. He seemed so lost and lonely – like a boat drifting on the sea. He could joke and smile, but the more I thought about it, the more it seemed like that was only on the surface. He was like the sea – the dancing surface glitteringly covered the dark depths. What was it that he was hiding? I was too young and knew he would never tell me, but I prayed that he would truly be happy. That Margaret would come back…that he would not feel cursed by the shipwrecks… that he would not be like the moody sea before a storm.

Chapter 15

I opened my eyes – awakened by a happy squeal. Marian kicked and played with her feet in her cradle box, and I leaned off the bed to tickle her chin. She reached up, begging to be held. I climbed out of bed, scooped her up, brushed the wispy hair out of my eyes, and eased open the closed door. The house was silent. Above me, Father was probably extinguishing the lamps. The boys huddled at the top of the stairs. Mama was not singing in the kitchen, and there was no sound of breakfast preparations. A graveyard-like silence reigned, and only the steady whisper of the sea proved it was not a dreamland. I shivered, afraid I knew what had happened.

The door to Uncle Richard's room stood ajar. Shifting Marian to my hip so I could hold her with one arm, I pushed the door. The wood creaked. Mama sat in a chair close to the bed; her head had fallen forward, and I thought she slept.

Uncle Richard turned his head on the pillow. His eyes were open, and he recognized us.

I felt dizzy for a moment in a surge of joy. He was alive. I wanted to dance and run up and down the stairs, shouting at the top of my voice, but I didn't want to scare him. "Is it alright?" he murmured. "Is there light? Did it shine through the night?"

Silent, I nodded, and he smiled drowsily.

Backing out of the room, I gathered the boys. When I told them the good news, they started hollering, but I shushed them quickly.

"He will get well?" Paul asked. I nodded again, smiling and afraid I'd cry. "That's good. He has a lot more songs to teach me to whistle."

Uncle Richard did get better. In the next few days, he recovered rapidly, and before long, Mama threatened to tie him in bed so he'd rest.

"I wish you would," he grumbled good-naturedly. "Then I could work at escaping instead of just laying here thinking."

"Did you want to write some epic poetry? It's a good cure for thinking," I suggested, having followed Mama, carrying a plate of bread while she balanced the soup bowl.

"What is wrong with thinking, you two?" Mama asked.

Uncle Richard sat up and leaned against his pillows. "When you have too many memories, it is possible to think too much."

"But…" I began.

"Susan, please go downstairs and finish setting the table," Mama said, interrupting my question.

I went, feeling shut out. I was only going to say something nice and positive. Why did Mama send me away and prevent me from commenting?

Sensing the dinner table wasn't a good place, I finally asked when Mama and I were washing the dishes. "Why didn't you let me talk to Uncle?"

"I thought you were going to ask an insensitive question."

"I thought it would be good to talk to him." Lifting a plate from the rinse water, I waited for Mama's answer.

She paused and sighed. "Do you see when his eyes are a stormy blue or the dull color of a foggy sea? He has had those expressions all his life, and as his younger sister, I quickly learned to leave him alone when he has those expressions."

I dried a plate with unnecessary energy. "Did he usually look like that?"

"No. Usually he was happy. There was light in his eyes, even if he wasn't smiling."

"Do you see that now?"

Mama shook her head. "No. Even when he's smiling, there's no light."

I snatched a plate, hoping to wipe away my confusion as easily as the water drops. "Why doesn't he talk to us?" I blurted. In my frustration, I practically scoured the already clean plate as if trying to peel away layers of secrets by fierce action. The plate slipped from my hands. It broke into two large pieces and tiny shards.

I bent down to pick up the large pieces, immediately feeling foolish. I had my own struggles I didn't want to talk about. Mama knelt beside me. "Because it's hard to mend what's broken," she said, answering my question. "And, Susan, if we try too hard or use force – we break things beyond repair. Do you understand what I'm saying?"

I nodded, but I didn't like it. I wanted to mend broken things for my uncle. Looking at the pieces of broken china, though, I knew I had to be more quiet and patient. I thought of Father's words after the inspector's lecture. Trust has to be earned, I remembered, and loyalty can't be bought. Loyalty – again.

I awoke the next day with the idea to put my thoughts into rhyme. The morning light filtered in at my bedroom window, and I watched the sea breaking on the rocks as I worked on the elegant phrasing.

> "Loyalty – where dost thou dwell?
> In wooded glen or ocean swell…"

Below, a door shut firmly, and glancing down, I saw Uncle Richard standing there. He haltingly walked to one of the barrels blossoming with summer flowers and carefully plucked a bouquet.

"A surprise for Mama?" I wondered. But he did not come back into the house. Instead, he rested a moment – obviously still weak from his illness – and then walked with reluctant steps toward the rocks. With one swift motion, he tossed the bouquet into the sea and bent his head.

I could imagine the sea tumbling the delicate flowers, pulling them away in a receding tide then casting them back with violent fury until the petals were broken. No longer anything more than faint fragments of their former beauty.

He stood there for a long time, looking down and not seeing the sun rise. I clutched my pencil, afraid of what he might be thinking. I wanted to go to him and make him tell us what was wrong, but I remembered the broken plate. Driving him away with nosy questions was not the way to earn trust.

I could start my chores early, I thought. I could begin by going to the shed to gather the eggs; Paul wouldn't mind if I took care of the pesky hens that supposedly always pecked him. I could call to my uncle and pretend like I hadn't seen him that morning. As if I didn't know he had thrown perfectly beautiful flowers into the ocean. That might work to distract him from whatever he was thinking…

When I slipped out the door with the basket, Uncle Richard had turned back toward the lighthouse, walking with his head bowed, shoulders slumped, and hands in his pockets. He looked so dejected that I ran to him.

"Uncle Richard," I said, not too brightly but in a cheerful tone. "Did you see the sunrise? It looks like the beginning of an even better day."

He looked at me and tried to smile, but I saw his eyes were red from tears. He quickly returned his gaze to the ground, starting to walk away. Show him you care, I thought. You can do it without a word. He had reached out to ask about my poetry when I was unhappy.

I walked beside him. All was silent except for the cries of the seabirds. I reached up and gently grasped his wrist, drawing his hand from his pocket. Wrapping my fingers around his hand, I hoped he knew he was not alone.

Chapter 16

I never finished the poem about loyalty. Uncle Richard and I didn't talk about that morning. When we reached the door, he said gruffly, "I'm fine," and at breakfast displayed his reserved good humor. In the next days, he played with the boys, teaching them how to make slingshots with wood, string, and a piece of thick cloth. For the first time, he played with Marian, using the reflection of a tiny pocket mirror to make faces while she squealed with laughter. He went for long walks and brought home beautiful sea shells or delicate bird feathers for me. He harvested the ripe garden vegetables for Mama. Half-way through the week, he took part of the night watch, and by the end of seven days, he was back to his regular lightkeeping routine which allowed Father to get more rest.

One morning Mama sent me upstairs to sweep the bedrooms. Mattie followed me from room to room, and in

Uncle Richard's room, she crawled under the bed and lay there poking her nose out to look at me. I leaned the broom against the wall, then raised and lowered the quilt. "Peek-a-boo," I teased her. Mattie twitched her nose and didn't seem impressed. She crawled farther under the bed while I raised the quilt to watch her.

Something hung like a hammock, slung close to the bed ropes underneath the mattress. I reached and tapped it. Hard, like a book. The hammock sling wasn't tight, and without thinking, I pulled out the object. A notebook of papers. I opened it, hardly knowing what I thought I'd find. Only navigational charts and a few maps. I'd always been terrible at geography so I didn't recognize much on the maps. I caught my breath. I was snooping! I snapped the book shut and replaced it exactly as I found it and lowered the quilt.

I sat on the floor, feeling shaky. I'd never done anything that naughty before. Crawling under a bed and snooping! That wasn't the way to gain anyone's trust. Loyalty and trust – that got me thinking. Why would Uncle Richard devise such a hiding place for a harmless book of charts and maps? Did he not trust us?

I puzzled over the issue of trust that afternoon as Mama and I worked on some sewing in the parlor while Marian took her nap. The boys wriggled at the dining table, finishing their schoolwork since they'd helped Father check the bird snares and fishing lines in the morning. They huffed and puffed because I didn't have to do schoolwork with them since I had finished my studies earlier. Mama sewed the long seams on new shirts for Father on her hand-crank sewing machine between telling the boys to sit up and finish their work.

I poked my needle in and out of the sampler cloth, making the stitched letters form my name above the stitched water and below the puffy clouds. We had to trust Uncle Richard, and he had to trust us. Father could have told the inspector about Uncle's mysterious past, but he didn't. Now, had I broken trust by not thinking about my actions?

The sewing machine whirling was punctuated with pauses and the energetic snip of Mama's scissors as she cut and tied the loose threads. I watched her work, mesmerized at how skillfully she guided the fabric under the dancing needle and how calmly she matched the seams. Mama brushed away some threads and folded the shirts; there was hand sewing to complete on them later. She leaned forward with a secret smile lighting her face. "Susan," she whispered as though she guarded a happy secret, "do you want to bake an apple pie to surprise your father? It's his favorite dessert."

"Really, Mama?" I exclaimed, dropping my needle in my excited response. When Jane, Anna, and I had played at keeping house, we always baked the most delicious imaginary pies and cakes. Now, it was finally time for me to start learning how to make the real desserts.

"Yes, I think it's time to improve your kitchen skills. Find your needle first and then come join me in the kitchen."

"Oh, but Mama...where will we find the apples?"

"Lesson one for improving your cooking skills: a good cook knows how to improvise. Lesson two: a thrifty woman can always make something special."

I searched and searched for that lost needle, running my hands over the wood floor. In my excitement, it seemed an eternity to find it, but I think it was only a minute or two before I found it beside the leg of the chair. Stabbing the needle into my folded sampler, I skipped through the main room and into the kitchen. "What are you doing?" the boys called after me.

"It's a surprise," I said, closing the kitchen door. "Don't peek."

Mama had set out a bowl and a rolling pin, and as I entered, she was placing another bowl covered with a towel on the center work table. "We don't have fresh apples right now. But dried apples work well if you soak them in water first. I've already done that, so now the apples and raisins are ready. I will tell you the next ingredients and how much we need, and you can add them to the bowl of fruit," she directed as she drained off the water.

I measured sugar, flour, cinnamon, and a pinch of cloves and stirred the fruit and spices. Mama assembled the dry ingredients for the pie crust and put some lard into the bowl. She showed me how to blend the flour and lard together to combine them evenly. "Work on that. It will take a little while. I'm going to start on the fish chowder and build up the fire to heat the oven."

A stiff breeze blew through the open window, sending the curtains fluttering like un-reefed sails. "That wind is getting much cooler," Mama remarked. "Autumn will be here soon."

I nodded. The flour and lard were sticky at first, and I felt clumsy, but I soon settled into the steady motion of rubbing the ingredients between my fingers. About the time I thought I was mastering the skill, Mama peered over my shoulder and said, "That looks perfect, Susan!" Next, we added some water, and Mama showed me how to stir and mix until the ingredients clung together as semi-sticky dough.

Mama rolled the bottom pie crust, explaining as she patted, floured, rolled, and turned the dough into a thin circle. Effortlessly, she pried it off the bread board and lined the pie pan. We added the apples and raisins. Then I tried my hand at rolling the top crust. It was hard! But Mama patiently guided me through the steps. The top crust cracked a little as I picked it up, but we repaired it, and it would still taste delicious. Mama showed me how to trim and crimp the edges and then slid the pie into the oven. I couldn't wait to see what Father thought at supper when he saw the surprise.

"Susan Rose's first apple pie," Father exclaimed, approvingly, as we brought the dessert to the table after supper. I carried a piece to him, and when everyone was served he took the first bite, closing his eyes. "Mmm…mmm," he intoned, "just delicious. In the next ten years, don't you be baking any pies for anyone except us, Susan Rose, or else I'll have to fight off the young men with a stick." He winked at me, and I squirmed, happily embarrassed at the idea that years down the road somebody might want to marry me 'cause I was a good cook.

"I think I have a lot more cooking and sewing to learn, Father," I replied, blushing.

"That you do, Susan Rose. And I'm glad."

"Don't ever go away," Jacob ordered. "You have to bake lots more pies for us."

Paul chimed in, "This is the best pie ever! Don't let Uncle Richard have a piece."

"That doesn't sound nice," I said. "He can have a piece when he has supper and Father takes the watch."

"I have a surprise too," Father announced, pushing away his empty plate. "Tomorrow we are going on a picnic."

"A picnic?" I asked. "With whom?" In past years, we went on picnics with our friends or our friends came to the lighthouse for the outing. Jane, Anna, and I had loved picnics; we would run and play with our siblings until we were hot and tired, then we'd sit near our mothers and try to look like calm, respectable ladies, usually making exaggerated dignified faces until we burst into giggles.

"Just us," Father explained, answering my question. "I found a nice sandy beach not too far away. Mama and I decided to make a holiday. We'll take the dory over to the beach, enjoy lunch, and spend a few hours exploring. It will likely be our last chance for such an excursion before the colder autumn weather begins."

"Yippee!" Jacob shouted.

Paul bounced in his seat, then stopped suddenly to ask, "Is Uncle Richard going?"

"Not this time," Father answered matter-of-factly. "Someone has to stay at the lighthouse. I talked with him, and he is fine with our plans."

"I can't wait," I exclaimed, thinking about how much fun we'd have tomorrow.

Later, as I watched Uncle Richard enjoy his piece of pie and tease me for a second piece, I tried to reconcile his new-found cheerfulness with his aloofness and secretive past. What would motivate a man to hide harmless sea charts as if they were a valuable treasure?

Then, too, what would motivate a girl to spend her spare moments writing poetry instead of facing realities properly? Were we only mirroring each other? Unknowingly?

Chapter 17

The next morning the boys and I hurried through our chores, and by half-past nine, we sat on the stairs, watching over the food basket, picnic blanket, bundle of shawls, and the canvas bag of games. It seemed like we waited forever, and we devised our own amusement.

"Trade hats with me," Jacob demanded, offering his cap and pointing at my straw hat decorated with yellow ribbons.

I shoved the cap over my braids at a silly angle. "You look ridiculous," Jacob laughed.

"So do you," I replied. "You look positively silly with all those ribbons. No, no, don't even tie it. Give it back, give it back."

Jacob removed my hat but refused to give it back. "Trade hats with me now, Paul."

"Oh, no," Paul responded virtuously as though he had never done anything childish in his life. "I am busy minding

Marian." He sat on the bottom stair while Marian clutched his knee and stood wobbling; he told her how to take her first steps, but she didn't seem eager to walk.

"Fine. I want my cap back, Susan," Jacob declared, and we exchanged hats again.

Father came down the stairs – scattering us from our seats – and Mama followed, carrying her newly re-finished straw bonnet. "Ready?" Father asked. "Grab something from the pile, and let's go. Think you can take care of the place all by yourself for a few hours, Richard?" he said teasingly as Uncle came down the stairs – book in hand – to see us off.

"Yep, don't worry. I won't snooze too much on the job." He grinned, then made a snoring sound which made Father look at him with mock alarm. "No, I've got a book that's too exciting to sleep through. What time will you be back?"

"By half-past three," Father replied.

"Bye," I called, scurrying out the door, toting the picnic blanket and clutching my notebook. It wouldn't be good to have ideas and no paper or pencil. I hoped even the short change of scenery would help me clear my thoughts of real-life secrets and give new writing inspiration.

At the dock, Father helped us into the small boat and placed all our baggage as a sort of ballast. After giving strict instructions not to move around too much and to keep our hands out of the water, he pushed away from the little dock and rowed with quick strokes. Mama sat in the stern, and I sat next to her, holding Marian and telling her about all the things we saw.

Uncle Richard had walked down to the rocks and waved at us as we went in the opposite direction, toward the beach Father had told us about. I felt a little bad for him and wished he could've come with us.

"Look, look," Paul squealed a few minutes later. "It's a seal." He pointed to a shadow swimming alongside the boat at a little distance.

"Where, where?" Jacob asked, leaning over.

Mama and I tried to point it out while Father paused rowing. Right then, the seal popped its head out of the water and looked in our direction with large curious eyes.

"He's waving," I exclaimed as the seal splashed his flipper. The seal followed us for a while, then waved his flipper again, and dove deep into the water.

Our boat moved smoothly past many pretty spots on the coast, but none was as beautiful as where Father directed the dory. It was a perfect beach, just like he said it would be, with a tiny, sheltered cove boarded by shallow water and a strip of soft sand. The grasses and shore bushes cropped up at a good distance from the water, and a couple of large rocks nestled at the far side, near where Father dragged the boat ashore.

Mama and I spread out the picnic blanket, and then I ran off to join my brothers. Jacob, Paul, and I played game of graces, tag, and hide-n-seek. Father joined us for a game of toss rings, which was something like horseshoes. Laughing and panting, we collapsed on the picnic blanket when Mama called us to come eat. She had opened the picnic basket and prepared a plate for each of us with a hard-boiled egg, bread with jam, slice of fried salt pork, and dried blueberries. For dessert: doughnuts!

After the meal, Father and the boys went exploring in the woods, and having brought a book, Mama said she would stay with Marian who was ready for a rest. I walked along the beach alone, watching the endless tide. Ahead, a gull skidded to an awkward landing. I ran at him, chasing him in good fun until he spread his wings and soared away, then wheeled high above me with a mocking screech. I smiled and ran, skipping down the shore and splashing in the foaming tide. Then I sobered. Only my shadow chased me. Not my brothers, not my friends.

Shadows, flitting in and around our lives. My uncle's secrets. My own lonely troubles. Mama's regretful confession. Even the boys had secret wishes. Only Father had not revealed a secret, but perhaps he kept one from Inspector Milton.

Combatting the shadows came truth, like our lighthouse's warning beams in the night. To survive at a lighthouse – Father had said – one had to rely on the best character qualities. Honesty, courage, hard-work, dedication, loyalty. I survived at the lighthouse by hiding my loneliness and struggles. Or did I really survive? Would there be fewer shadows if we whole-heartedly embraced the principles of lightkeeping into our own lives?

Lulled and wearied by these answerless thoughts, I soon became tired and wandered back to lie on the blanket. The sun's warmth banished the gloominess, and I dozed, listening to the sound of the waves and dreaming of my friends.

As the sun moved closer to the inland horizon, we headed back to the lighthouse in the boat. Nearing home, we were surprised to see a horse and small carriage standing in the yard. "I suppose we have guests," Father remarked. "I don't think the inspector would come again so soon. Unless…"

I shivered. Unless Inspector Milton had uncovered a secret that might call into question my uncle's ability as an assistant lightkeeper.

"Of all the days for visitors," Mama sighed. "Well, at least the house is clean, and I'm sure Richard is capable of giving a tour and being hospitable."

As soon as we reached the top of the path from the dock, Uncle Richard rushed out the kitchen door and hurried toward us. His sleeves were rolled up, his hair looked like he'd run his hands through it, and there was a worried expression on his face. "Thank goodness you're home, Harriet. A gentleman and his daughter came to the lighthouse, arriving about an hour ago. I showed them around, and then I offered to make some tea, but the water isn't boiling, and I couldn't find the good dishes. And I have this awful feeling they are watching me even now and laughing at my troubles."

"There now," Mama replied. "If you built up the fire well – which I'm sure you did – then you just have to wait for the kettle to sing. And a watched kettle never boils. Why don't you go and entertain the guests with a story or two? I'll make the tea, and you can introduce us."

He sighed in great relief. "Thank goodness. I'd rather navigate the Diamond Shoals than fail at serving tea to that lady."

I frowned as I entered the kitchen, imagining a haughty lady who would look down her nose at me and make some remark about my supposedly wretched uncultured life at a lighthouse. Father had already gone into the parlor, and we children followed after we had washed our hands and faces. Reluctantly, I stepped into the room.

Near the parlor window stood a young lady with laughing blue eyes, silky golden curls, and a bright smile. Her gown was dark blue and white striped, and she wore a fascinatingly tiny blue hat, slid forward on her brow. My uncle was stammering some apology about tea as we entered, but she brushed aside his embarrassment with an airy motion of her gloved hand, saying delightedly, "Oh, please, Mr. Bates, don't trouble yourself on our account."

"Indeed," said the well-dressed gentleman seated in one of the comfortable chairs, "we are in no hurry. And I'm sure you would've managed just fine, or you could've always asked Elsie to help you. Though she looks like a doll, she is quite resourceful and knowledgeable in housekeeping."

Uncle Richard looked more uncomfortable and tugged at the cuff of his coat. He saw us, smiled gratefully, and introduced us to the guests. "My nieces, Susan and Marian. My nephews, Jacob and Paul. Children, this is Mr. Shermann and his daughter, Miss Elsie Shermann."

"How do you do?" I responded, curtsying a little. Marian smiled and wriggled, anxious to get down and crawl on the floor.

"Well. Well, indeed. Any day by the sea is a real blessing," Mr. Shermann said. "I'm an artist, and the sea is my inspiration. No cities for me. And no prisons and hospitals either. Though having seen darkness, it is easier to find and paint light." I looked at him more observantly, noticing an empty left sleeve pinned to the front of his coat and the faint traces of a sickly pallor on his face. His blue eyes were like the sky after a storm and the ends of his drooping mustache rose as he smiled. "And Elsie comes with me in my travels. She says it's good for her writing," he finished proudly.

"Papa, you shouldn't," she said gently. "Not everyone thinks writing is a proper pastime for a lady."

"I myself can't think of any objections," Uncle Richard announced; he looked so charming and agreeable that I had to try not to laugh. Could my uncle be falling in love with this lady so quickly? Father must have seen the expression too because he asked if Uncle Richard had finished the lightkeeping chores.

When Uncle Richard turned to answer Father, Miss Elsie's sweet smile darkened for an instant, and she seemed to be watching Uncle Richard closely. The change was hardly noticeable, but I saw it, and the watchfulness in her eyes made me shiver.

Mama entered with a tray – tea pot, cups, and a small plate of doughnuts. She directed us children to go and put away our toys from the picnic and start our afternoon chores.

Later, when I found Mama in the kitchen and began collecting the dishes to set the table, she said, "Mr. and Miss Shermann will be joining us for supper. Please be sure to set the extra places."

"Will they be leaving after supper?" I asked, worried about that expression I'd seen on Miss Shermann's face and suddenly not sure if Uncle Richard should like this lady.

"No, they will be staying. Mr. Shermann wants to paint and has asked to stay here for a couple days. So we will be hospitable. Uncle Richard and the boys will give up their rooms. Jacob and Paul will sleep on pallet beds in your room, and Richard will sleep downstairs. That way our guests will have comfortable accommodations," Mama explained.

"Who are they?" I insisted.

"A wealthy businessman and his daughter. He was apparently a soldier during the war and is now an artist. She is a writer."

"Mama, what if they are not who they seem?" But Mama had bustled into the pantry and didn't hear my question.

Chapter 18

"Miss Shermann," I said as I guided her up to her room after the evening meal, "what do you write? If you don't mind my question." She had perfect manners and the most fascinating way of controlling the conversation at the table, without seeming to be in charge.

"It depends," she replied, smiling. "Sometimes short stories. Sometimes information about travel or the impracticality of these beautiful ladies' fashions. Anything I can sell to a newspaper or magazine. Oh, and calling me Miss Elsie is fine."

"You write for a living?" I responded, a little awed.

"Not really for a living. More for fun. And you are one of the few people outside a literary circle who think that's a good thing."

As I lay in bed, listening to my brothers whisper, I wondered what my uncle thought about such a friendly young lady and her father. He didn't seem to know them from the past. In fact, he might actually like the young lady, which wasn't a bad thing as long as she wasn't hiding a harmful secret.

"What do you think, Mattie?" I asked, stroking the cat's fur the next morning as she perched on the windowsill. I had just finished cleaning my bedroom, folding up the boys' pallet beds, and sweeping the floor. The busy day had started early as usual, but I discovered that our guests were even earlier risers. They did not join us for breakfast since Mr. Shermann was already out near the rocks at work at his sturdy easel while Miss Elsie sat in a low chair close beside him. The day was autumn cool, but the sun shone brightly.

"Should I?" I questioned Mattie again. "It doesn't seem fair to suspect someone of something bad because of one cross look." In the end, I decided to watch and see what happened during the day. Hours later, Mama told us we could go outside and play. After putting my school books and slate on the shelf, I got my hat and skipped outside.

Miss Elsie saw me and waved. The boys ran off to play with the goats, but I went to where the authoress sat. She closed her folder and smiled up at me as I greeted her. "Please thank your mother again for allowing me to bring lunch to Papa out here while he is working. He can be very preoccupied when he's creating art. Will you sit with me for a little while?"

"What is he doing today?" I asked, sitting down on a large rock.

"Drawing with pencil. That's how he gets his ideas, and it also allows him to watch the lighting at a location. Tomorrow he wants to start painting. And tomorrow I will start writing. I've thought of several good ideas."

"You find good ideas really easily," I complimented.

"I'm thinking about an article on lighthouse keepers. What if I use your father and uncle as the unnamed models for my article? What do you think? Did they have exciting lives before they settled into lightkeeping?"

I frowned at her question and watched a couple waves tumble on the rocks before replying. "My father did. He worked on a whaling ship." I shrugged, determined to be careful. "I don't know much about my uncle's life."

"Is he a war veteran? My papa always tells me to be sure to highlight war records in my writing." She asked with such innocence that for a moment I wondered if I'd been mistaken in my unknown suspicions. She really could be just a writer who was suddenly interested in my uncle.

"He hasn't told us any war stories." That was true. "Our lighthouse is not really near a town. How did you know to come here?"

"Well, Papa is always looking for new scenes to paint, and when our friend – Inspector Milton – told us that Herdman Point Lighthouse is one of the best and prettiest lights on this part of the Long Island Sound, we just had to come."

"You know Inspector Milton, then?" I questioned.

"Oh, yes. I attended finishing school with his youngest daughter and have remained good friends with her and her family through the last few years."

I really didn't think she was lying, but I worried. Too many pieces fit into the puzzle. I had to tell someone before Miss Shermann caused any trouble.

"What do you do in your spare time here at the lighthouse?"

I'd never tell her my secret or about my writing; there was something wrong with her niceness and questions. "Schoolwork, chores, sewing, helping Mama. There's always lots to do. In fact, Mama asked me to help her with supper preparations. We are planning to eat earlier so my father and uncle can join us before the night watches. Won't you excuse me?" I rose and walked toward the lighthouse, willing myself not to run.

Inside, I found Father, polishing brass in the workroom. I closed the door, saying, "I need to talk to you."

"So serious?" Father teased. "What? Did you find a mouse that Mattie missed?"

"No, listen, please. I've been talking with Miss Shermann. I think she's a spy. I think she's spying on Uncle Richard. We have to tell him."

I explained the whole story to Father, but he seemed doubtful and very reluctant to tell Uncle Richard. "It's probably nothing. I don't want him to panic. And it might not be a bad thing if he courted a nice lady. I think you hinted at that yourself a few months ago."

"But what if she's not nice? Shouldn't we warn him? Maybe he should at least be careful of what he says?"

"Your uncle didn't say much last evening, and I don't suppose he'll reveal his whole life history to a stranger."

"Does he like her, Father?"

"I'll keep an eye on him, Susan Rose. Don't worry."

I didn't worry until I saw Mr. Shermann and his daughter walking toward the lighthouse. Peeping through one of the front windows, I watched Uncle Richard coming up from the dock, carrying a torn fish net. He handed it to the boys, tagging along behind him, then smoothed his wind-tangled hair and greeted the guests. Miss Elsie let him carry her chair and looked at him with an unforgettably bright smile. They seemed to chat playfully as they came toward the door, and I wished Father could see this.

At supper, I watched Uncle Richard carefully as he sat across from me and beside the boys. He paid attention to the food on his plate and avoided looking at Miss Elsie who sat to my right. She glanced frequently in his direction and also kept a watchful eye on Father who sat at the head of the table.

Mr. Shermann seemed inclined to talk, and Father asked about his artwork after the food had been served. He smiled, replying, "Well, I like the lighting and think I will be able to complete two paintings in the next three days."

"So quickly, Papa?" Miss Elsie questioned. "It's so pleasant here. I truly will be sorry to leave."

"They will not be quite as detailed as my previous work. But I think I will be able to convey the right image and feeling."

"How do you paint a feeling?" Jacob asked, setting down his cup a little too noisily.

"It's more of what I want someone to think or feel when they look at the artwork."

"Oh. Um, alright," Jacob said with a tiny shrug.

"How long have you been painting, Mr. Shermann?" Mama asked as she finished spreading jam on a piece of bread for Paul.

"About a year and a half. I started as I recovered from the war."

"Tell them, Papa," Miss Elsie urged.

He took a deep breath. "There isn't much to tell. I was and am a shareholder in a railroad company. When the war came, I waited. Didn't enlist for two years, thinking it'd all be over soon. But then there was the draft. I was too patriotic to buy a substitute to go in my place. I decided to go. Serve my country." Mr. Shermann glanced down, hesitating.

"Went to war. Just in time for the Overland Campaign – Grant versus Lee in '64." He closed his eyes. "Got shot in the arm. Taken prisoner by the Confederates. Days later, they got around to giving me medical care: amputation. I lost my left arm, as you see. Without proper time to rest or recover, I was sent to prison. I don't remember where, but it was an unhealthy place, and I was sick for months. Lost track of time completely. Hunger, fever, pain, and loneliness were the only things I knew. An imprisoning darkness. And then one day they told me I was free." He shook his head slowly. "Free," he repeated.

"I found him and brought him to a military hospital – actually the one I'd been volunteering at for several months," Miss Elise finished, touching her father on the shoulder.

Mr. Shermann added, "And it's been a long road to recovery. But with strengthened faith, my daughter's patience, and learning to find beautiful things to chase away the ugly memories, I think I will come through this a stronger man."

There was a hush around the table. Mr. Shermann had told the story simply but with so much emotion. I sensed the darkness in his story and thought he reached desperately for the light. I believed him and felt he meant no harm.

To break the tension, Mr. Shermann said with forced cheerfulness. "Now, now, enough about me. Surely some of you have a better war story. Come, tell all."

Father shook his head. "No, no stories like yours. I would've joined, but the Lighthouse Board and the District Inspector told me it would be best to tend and guard the light. There were a few uneasy nights because of the Confederate spies and feared sabotage. But nothing serious was officially reported in our area."

"You never told us about it, Father," I said.

"There wasn't any reason to scare you."

"Were there really Rebels on the Lakes?" Jacob asked, wide-eyed.

"Yes. Some escapades made it to the newspapers. I'm sure many things happened that were never reported."

"What would have happened if Confederates came to your lighthouse, Mr. Arnold?" Miss Elsie asked, picking up her knife with a firm gesture. She asked Father the question, but looked at Uncle Richard as she spoke. He remained expressionless.

"That would have depended on many things," Father answered. "There was always the possibility that U.S. troops could have defended the structure if they arrived in time. I could've defended it, or I could've been taken prisoner, or we could've fled. It of course depended on the actual situation, but thankfully that didn't happen."

"Wow, Father," Jacob said. "I didn't know that."

"They can't come get you now, can they?" Paul asked, watching the windows for an unseen enemy.

"We didn't talk about it because we didn't want you children to be afraid. No, Paul, you are safe here."

Father and I looked at each other. He was calm, but I wanted to stand up and tell him Miss Elsie was asking too many questions. Then I felt torn – maybe I was wrong? Maybe she was just a nice lady, interested in everyone's stories.

"And you, Mr. Bates," Miss Elsie began, looking toward Uncle Richard, "were you involved in the late war?" I watched her hands on the utensils and noticed her grip tighten as she smiled innocently.

Uncle Richard helped himself to another piece of fish, then answered, "I was in Scotland for many of those years. I worked at a chandlery building. We may have occasionally outfitted blockade runners, but it was not my place to inquire too closely. Work is work. The politics of the jobs were the shop owners' concerns."

"Blockade runners? Tell us more, please," Paul requested, leaning around Jacob to see Uncle Richard.

"Blockade runners, eh? They were the supply line to the Confederate States after the Union navy attempted to block entrance and exit from the Southern ports. They brought weapons, medicines, and diplomatic messages in – along with frivolous items for the rich – and they took out the cotton. Some ran straight to Europe, but most sailed for the Bahamas or West Indies in an attempt to lose any Union ships trailing them. Some exchanged cargo on the islands and went straight back, others went to Europe from there."

I wanted to scream "stop," but I couldn't. I thought he was telling too much that might be connected with his past, and there was a stranger in the room. What if Miss Elsie was one of those people who knew something about his mysterious past? What if she was one of the people he thought couldn't find him at the lighthouse? But what if this was just information that he knew through a friend? I still didn't know what to believe, but I did not like the situation.

"Where in Europe did the blockade runners go?" Jacob asked.

"France, England, Scotland, Ireland, mostly."

"Did they ever get caught?" Jacob wondered.

Uncle Richard paused. "Yes, of course." His voice was overly careless. "But many did make it."

"What would a captain do if he was being chased?" Paul asked.

"Either run for the shore, praying to find a good inlet. Or turn back to sea, hoping not to meet another Union warship."

"Did you ever hear a good story when you were working at the chandlery? I mean, if a blockade runner came to be refitted," Miss Elsie asked, apparently quite interested in the account.

"Oh, there was one fellow who came in. He'd made two good voyages and had got a small fortune for his success. But he wasn't lucky on that last run."

"What happened?"

"A storm wrecked the ship."

"Did he survive?" Miss Elsie asked, leaning forward slightly.

"He is alive," Uncle Richard replied shortly. "But…he has…well, he didn't seem the same. Losing ships can have bad effects."

"Well, I hope his good fortune will return," Mr. Shermann said.

"I don't think." He stopped. "I don't know. He was an acquaintance."

I kicked Father's chair, and he looked at me, puzzled. The clock made its whirling sound from the parlor, getting ready to strike. Mama glanced around the table and offered more food to our guests. Miss Elsie declined the offer and settled into her chair, looking like she was quite pleased with herself.

A moment later Miss Elsie asked an odd question with probing energy, "Mr. Bates, are you certain he was just an acquaintance?"

"Yes, I am quite sure. I don't talk about the war. Please excuse me, Miss Shermann, Mr. Shermann. I have the early watch on the light and need to attend to my duties."

As Miss Elsie started chatting with Mama, I whispered to Father, "She knows whatever she needed to know. She's too happy."

He smiled indulgently and shook his head.

Chapter 19

The following day at the breakfast table, Mr. Shermann said, "Mr. Bates, your story last evening? My sister and her family moved to Scotland a few years ago. I wonder if you ever met them."

"Oh, Papa," Miss Elsie interrupted, "I can't imagine what a fellow working in a chandlery would've known about my cousins." She had hardly paid any attention to Uncle Richard this morning.

"Nevertheless, I still wonder. Their last name is Jamison. Were you acquainted with them, Mr. Bates?"

I felt like someone had forced all the air out of my lungs. This time I'd know if Uncle Richard lied – assuming it was the same family. He had a woman's portrait labeled M. Jamison.

Uncle Richard delayed his reply a little too long but answered, "I was acquainted. The owner of the shop where I was employed seemed well acquainted with Mr. Jamison."

Across the table, Miss Elsie laid down her utensils. Her blue eyes filled with tears, and she pushed away from the table. "Oh – please excuse me." Her swift footsteps echoed as she went upstairs. I didn't think she was acting that time.

An hour later Miss Elsie had gone out with her father, and I trudged up and down the stairs, emptying the water basins. "Susan Rose, come up here," Father called from the lantern. I climbed to the watchroom, then up the ladder into the glass-walled room. The clouds and sun played hide-n-seek that day, making the room first bright, then shadowy again.

"Uncle Richard wants to know if we know anything about Miss Shermann. I don't, but you had that conversation with her. Would you tell us about it?"

"I'm afraid it's too late," I admitted, "but I'll tell you what I know. Uncle Richard, at the beginning of summer, I overheard you telling Father that no one at the lighthouse could know about a secret, and that no one in the outside world knew where to find you. I'm sorry. I know I probably shouldn't have heard that, but you were talking loudly in the watchroom."

"Nevermind. You don't know anything you shouldn't know," Uncle Richard said, leaning forward with an alert expression I hadn't seen before. "Go on."

I told them about Miss Elsie's questions for her article. "Odd, but probably harmless," Father commented, but my uncle shook his head.

"She's acquainted with Inspector Milton. He told them to come here since it's a well-run lighthouse and pretty location,"

Father said, after he heard those details. "Nothing too sinister there, is there?"

Uncle Richard ran his hands through his hair, then smashed his fist into his palm. "Why didn't you tell me this when it first happened? I would've done things differently had I known."

"I didn't want to upset you," Father admitted. "What's going on?"

"Look. I can't tell you. Now, I have to decide what to do. Of course, it might already be done, noticing her reaction this morning."

"If you're not going to tell us, don't talk out loud," Father advised in a frustrated tone.

For two more days, Miss Elsie and Uncle Richard politely avoided and ignored each other. Or they tried to ignore each other. I caught Uncle Richard watching Miss Elsie when she was busy, and she did the same when she thought he was preoccupied. She pitied him in her expressions, and I couldn't help thinking it was because she was going to somehow ruin his life. In the evenings, Uncle Richard evaded conversation by going up to the watchroom early.

On the final day of the Shermanns' visit, an odd confrontation happened between my uncle and our pretty guest while I pulled up the dying flowers in the front barrel planters. On the front steps of the lighthouse, they collided, she trying to enter, he exiting.

Both in a hurry, they bumped into each other, mumbled apologies, tried to step out of the other's way and collided again. Then they stood there staring at each other, both expressionless. "Don't," he said, using a commanding tone.

"Don't what?" she taunted. "You'll have to be more specific. Pity you? Tattle on you? Don't what?"

"You know exactly, Miss Shermann."

"What do you think I know?" she retorted.

"Same question to you."

"More than I wanted to know about my cousins."

"How well could I have known that family if I was working in a chandlery shop?"

"Were you working in a chandlery shop?"

"Yes. Would you like me to repeat the catalog of goods for sale from memory? That's not something a man would memorize for fun. Miss Shermann, did it ever occur to you that you might have confused me for someone else?"

"Person: no. Character: maybe."

"What about yourself? Were you really a nurse during the war?"

"Would you like me to describe the precise steps for… stopping a secondary hemorrhage from an amputation? I don't believe that is something a lady would memorize to delight the evening guests. Anything else?"

"I don't think so, except I believe you have as many gray dresses as blue dresses. Perhaps even a blue dress covering gray petticoats, and a gray dress covering blue petticoats – depending on the place, time, and company. Be careful, Miss Sherman, lest you trip in your fine hoop and expose it all."

"Fine," she answered, losing her cool expression for the first time. "Let me go..."

Uncle Richard grasped her by the shoulders, "And you'll remember this moment. If it slips your mind, you'll regret it." He let her go, and she swept past him into the house, latching the door softly like a parting word.

"You're wondering what that was," Uncle Richard said, sitting on the steps and seeing me standing there with the dried plant stems in my hands. "Well, you were the chaperone witness that nothing bad happened. We just talked."

"But I didn't understand. What did you talk about?"

"That's because those kinds of conversations are best kept between the two who are talking. I don't think you'll need to worry about Miss Shermann giving anyone a bad report on me."

Later that evening I thought Mr. Shermann certainly wouldn't give us a bad report. As he displayed his small paintings, he kept praising and thanking our family for the hospitality, kindness, and good meals. The two paintings captured Herdman Point Lighthouse in the morning and at sunset. Both were pretty, but I liked the sunset one better; it seemed more accurate with the play of shadows and light on the building.

The next day the Shermanns left in their little carriage. They thanked my parents for their hospitality. Curiously, I watched Uncle Richard shake hands with Mr. Shermann, wishing him safe travels. Miss Elsie stood by her father and shook Uncle Richard's hand. "Good-bye," she said, trying to sound superior. "Come visit us at our home, if you like. You must come and tell us more about the blockade runners."

Uncle Richard released her hand quickly. "It is not likely I will ever discuss that with you again by choice, Miss Shermann. Good-bye." Turning abruptly, she climbed gracefully into the small carriage and snapped open her parasol. Mr. Shermann clucked to the gentle horse and held the reins firmly in his hand. Miss Elsie sat straight and proud; she did not look back.

"Too bad she wasn't as nice as she was pretty," I murmured.

"Oh, but she is," Uncle Richard assured me. "She's just very confused right now."

"Wait. Is she dangerous or not? You should at least be able to tell me that."

"I can't tell you that either because I don't know yet. We gave her a lot to think about."

"I don't understand this. And I don't want to!" I marched inside, leaving Uncle Richard to brood or rejoice however he saw fit. As for me, an imaginary world of princesses and knights seemed much more inviting at the moment.

Chapter 20

"I have a new secret," Paul announced to all of us at the dinner table.

Father laughed. "A secret you're going to tell us?"

Paul nodded. "It was too hard to whisper in everybody's ear last time. So I guess I'll tell you all now." He waited dramatically to make sure he had full attention. "I'm going to be a spy when I grow up."

"Are you indeed?" Uncle Richard asked.

"Were you a spy?" I questioned him.

"No."

"That sounds very interesting, Paul," Mama said. "What are you going to do when you're a spy?"

"I'm going to stop the bad men. And I'm going to take papers."

"Take papers?" Father questioned. "What does that mean?"

"You know," Paul started to get giggly.

"No, I don't know," Uncle Richard said with interest.

Through his laughter, Paul choked out, "Like Miss Elsie. I was hiding behind the door, and I saw her." Father and Uncle Richard looked at each other.

"Where did Miss Elsie take papers from?" Father questioned.

Paul stopped laughing and looked frightened by the serious tone. "Father's desk." Uncle Richard breathed a sigh of relief, but Father gripped the table. Both of them headed for the desk, Paul watching round-eyed at what his news had caused.

We stood in the parlor doorway while Father and Uncle Richard searched the desk. "Everything's here," Uncle Richard said. "Are you sure, Paul?"

He solemnly nodded. "She took something the first day she was here. Then later she went back, but I watched her all the time, and I didn't see her take anything else."

Father opened the top drawer and pressed along the upper structure. A panel dropped down from the drawer's ceiling. "No, it's gone."

"I don't understand," Uncle Richard said.

"It was a separate record book," Father admitted reluctantly. "On?"

The head lightkeeper and assistant lightkeeper looked at each other for an explosively silent moment. "I see," Uncle Richard finally said. "Trust is earned, eh?"

That's when I realized Father had a secret. A secret that could ruin Uncle Richard. Gasping, I turned and ran to my room. I lay on my bed, blinded by tears. I wished we'd never come here. Old complaints – which I'd tucked neatly behind me for so long – came charging back. Just when it felt like we were all starting to move in the same direction, everything fell apart. It was a different type of lonely ache this time. Sure, I still missed Jane and Anna, but I realized this time my lonely longing was for what might have been in my family. But our secrets had finally torn it apart. Probably forever. How could trust be earned and loyalty regained in this situation?

I tried to write poetry to forget the troubles, but this time it only made me feel more miserable. Mama came in and tried to talk to me, but I felt too heart-sad to listen to any explanations or plans. Then she wanted me to talk, but I shook my head. There was no reason to cause any more pain for anyone else.

The next morning everyone silently ate breakfast and went about their chores to avoid each other. I cornered Uncle Richard in the storage room. "You're not going to resign, are you?"

"Little other choice, especially when your 'captain' keeps a log book of the 'lieutenant's' moods, attitudes, and work."

"But you always did your work well. Father defended you in front of Inspector Milton."

"It doesn't erase the mistrust. And the fact that the book will be used against me now that Miss Shermann has it."

"Not if you tell the truth," I pleaded. "What made you so unhappy in the first place?"

"It's too complex, and no one would believe me anyway."

"You never gave them a chance, Uncle."

He reached under the workbench, yanked a canvas sling from a secretive hiding place, and stalked out of the room. He did not see the envelope flutter out of the canvas and land on the floor.

An irresistible pull like a wayward tide drew my hand to the weathered envelope, and impulsively, I took it and drew out a folded page, opening it and leaning toward the window light.

May 7, 1865
London, England
Dearest Richard,

We received your letter, and though it has caused us deep pain, never think for a moment that we blame you. You did everything you could to take care of her. What happened was an act of Providence, and you must not take a burden of guilt upon yourself.

She was never a girl who shied from adventure, and she always said she would follow her heart. Nothing you could have said or done would have prevented her from going.

We wish we could be with you. Come join us if you can. With the war over, we will stay where we are for now. Our door is open to you. Despite our former disagreements, you will always be regarded as our son.

Yours truly,
A.F.J and Family

I had found another secret…and again I wished I hadn't.
My hands trembled. I took a gulp of air as if I had been
drowning and drifting underwater. A lady had died while she
was a passenger on his ship? An English lady?

The lady must have drowned when Uncle Richard lost
his ship on the lake. No wonder he thought he was unlucky
and cursed. Why didn't he tell us? Was self-imposed guilt
the reason for his secrecy and occasional gloom? The family
seemed to have forgiven him and tried to comfort him. Why
couldn't he let the past go? Why did he think Father and even
the inspector wouldn't understand his unhappiness over this
tragic event?

I wished I hadn't seen the note. Hadn't thoughtlessly
opened and read it. It was my uncle's secret, and now I
desperately wanted to know more. Wanted more than ever to
help him. Whoever the writer was – probably someone in the
woman's family – did not blame my uncle for losing the ship
in the violence of the lake storm. I shivered as my imagination
wondered with horror at the thought of a woman drowning
in that rough water.

What was her name? Margaret. Margaret Jamison. The
lady in the picture. Was she related to Miss Elsie? What was that
connection? I reconstructed the details fancifully, imagining
a fearless woman who'd traveled to America in search of
adventure. Maybe she was a poet seeking new horizons. And
she wanted to see the heart of the lake…to understand the
beauty and power of the water…so she persuaded my uncle
who she met somewhere, somehow, and he agreed to let her

come. On a merchant ship, she would not be bothered by the social dictations of a passenger vessel and could focus on her writing. Then a storm came up, and she was so thrilled to stand in the spray, but she slipped and fell into the lake and in the process of trying to rescue her, someway, somehow, the ship sank, and my uncle felt cursed.

Deep inside, I knew something was wrong with the image I was creating. Was passion for writing really strong enough to compel a woman to take passage on a rough boat? Would any lady have traveled alone or did she have a chaperone who also could not prevent the accident? Would my uncle even have allowed such passengers on his ship? Still, it seemed possible and not a reason for Uncle Richard to spend his life in the unhappy shadows. If only he could explain the simple truth.

I paced in the workroom, replaying that evening conversation when Miss Elsie was here and when they were talking about blockade runners. Then I knew. My uncle had been a Confederate. A Rebel. The lady drowning in the Great Lake might have made him unhappy, but it was the war which made him prisoner. Somehow.

I remembered my musings on shadows and secrets and realized now that there were larger shadows than the ones we created on our lives. The war overshadowed us, even though it was over. I sensed a tie between my uncle's secrets and the war. Father never explained if the war had touched the Great Lakes, but – perhaps, just perhaps – something that happened there had prompted his seemingly senseless logbook on Uncle Richard. Clearly, that conflict haunted many lives. I thought about Anna's brother struggling to find joy and meaning in his life when he came home, both legs shot away. I remembered the crumpling, sobbing faces of the widows in church. The story of Mr. Dunbar who hurt Mattie and drank madly, trying to drowned his own war horrors. And I thought of Mr. Shermann painting to forget his hurts and injustices while his daughter tried to continue the pains caused by the conflict.

Chapter 21

Two uncomfortable days after the discovery that the papers were missing, a boy came to the lighthouse, riding a tired-looking mule. "Telegram for you. And they said I had to bring it all the way out here." Father handed over the coins, offered the boy some water, and sent him on his way. He left the opened telegram on the dining room table and went out to walk by the rocks.

Mama read it next, then returned to the kitchen and started pounding her bread dough with unnecessary energy. Uncle Richard read it and stomped upstairs. The boys and I leaned on the table, and I read the short message in a whisper.

I am coming to speak with keeper and assist. keeper as soon as practicable. Displeased.
Inspector T. Milton
US Lighthouse Inspector

"Is this because I told about the desk?" Paul asked with a quivering lip.

"No," Jacob said. "It's because Miss Elsie took the papers."

No, I thought to myself, it's because Father and Uncle Richard both have secrets and neither will confess. I didn't know what Father's secret was, but I knew enough about Uncle Richard's to say something.

I took the telegram and marched upstairs, stopping in my room to get the letter Uncle Richard had dropped the other day. Inwardly, I felt terrified, but that fear and anger combined to force me forward. I pounded on Uncle Richard's closed door. "Please let me in. I have to talk to you."

"Door's open," he said gruffly, and I flung it open.

"You have to tell them. Please. Father's going to lose his job, and you are too. Because both of you aren't telling the whole truth. And don't tell me nobody will be believe the truth if you haven't told it."

"Not a respectful way to speak, young lady. You might have a secret or two of your own, I'm guessing." He sat on the stool in the corner, holding one of his boots and a polishing cloth. After glancing at me, he continued shining his boot.

His calmness irritated me. "Uncle Richard, you have to tell them about the lady who drowned in Lake Michigan. Father and the inspector will understand why that makes you upset."

"The lady who drowned in the lake?" he questioned, looking up with a mystified expression

I held up the letter as proof. "You dropped this. And if you were a Confederate, you'd better tell them that too. I won't hate you ever. Even if you were a Rebel."

"If you want me to tell the truth, maybe you shouldn't invent it for me."

That wasn't the ending or answer I expected, and after a mumbled "sorry," I retreated to the watchroom, feeling more confused than before.

That afternoon Father said he was going for a walk in the woods to think for a while. "There may be a storm coming in, but I'm sure I'll be back before it arrives." Taking his hat, he went out.

Two hours later, the wind started rising, and dark clouds rolled in. Jacob and I ran to the shed to make sure the goats were warm and had some extra food. The squally wind was cold, and I held my shawl over my hair and ears for more warmth.

Uncle Richard came down from his room. "Better batten down the hatches," he said. "It's definitely getting colder, and I don't like the looks of the sky."

"Do you think Samuel will get home before the storm hits?" Mama asked, looking up from stirring the soup. "I wonder that he didn't notice the storm signs and come back sooner. He wouldn't leave the light, especially during a storm, no matter how upset he is. A sudden storm like this can catch mariners unaware and not give them much time to seek a harbor. I hope he gets back safely."

Uncle Richard unrolled his sleeves and buttoned the cuffs. "I'm going to light the lamps. May Susan help me?" Mama agreed.

My uncle carried the can of oil and asked me to bring the wick trimmers and matches. "The light is always prepared to be lit at any time," he explained as we climbed. "But just in case we need to fix something."

"I don't know how to help," I admitted. "Father promised to teach me everything when I turn eleven next year."

"It's alright. I know what to do." His words reassured me. Despite all his secrets, he had earned my trust that he could tend the light, even if he didn't let light into his own life.

I shivered as we climbed the ladder and emerged into the lantern. Watching the rough sea, I wondered again what might have prompted the woman to get on a ship. That woman who had died and whose family had written to my uncle. Was it something about the water that fascinated her? Or – likely – was it something stronger, more dear or important?

Already the sky darkened, and sprinkles of rain hit the glass windows. The natural light had a grayish green eeriness. The darkness crept in, trying to lure a ship onto the rocks. Only our light could warn of the nearby danger. I prayed Father would hurry home.

Working quickly and with no time to explain, Uncle Richard checked the lens and the lamps. Striking a match, he reached inside and lit the wicks. "Whew!" he exclaimed as the lamps blazed and the unlocked lens began revolving in a slow circle. "Better with the light, eh?"

I nodded, marveling at how it chased away the gloomy fears and approaching darkness. There was something inwardly thrilling about watching the match touch the lamp wick and seeing the light spring to life. "Come, we must go down," Uncle Richard said. "The light is too bright and could hurt our eyes if we stay here long."

We went down to the watchroom, and looking out the window, I saw Father hurrying toward the door. I ran downstairs and met him in the entry hall. "Father! You're home," I exclaimed, "and safe." Nothing could steal the thankfulness of that moment. Mama hugged him, despite his dripping, soaked coat.

"There now. Did you think I wasn't coming back? I had walked farther than I thought, so it took longer to get back." Outside the wind's howl rose another notch. "It will be a bad night on the sea for any ships out there. I'm glad Richard got the light lit early. I'll go up and thank him." His words introduced a truce as he headed upstairs to check the light for himself. While the keeper and assistant keeper's relationship was still far from cordial and ideal, I at least hoped there wouldn't be silent division.

After supper, Father went up to check the light and talk to Uncle Richard again, then returned to sit in his rocking chair. Marian climbed in his lap and played with her doll. The boys tried to play a game of rule-less checkers, but neither was very attentive, distracted by big yawns and the storm. I watched the firelight and tried to finish a poem, thinking it was a dull evening and wondering how long until bedtime. The storm and early darkness seemed to make us drowsy.

Suddenly, we heard Uncle Richard running down the stairs. "All hands on deck," he shouted. "There's a ship in danger. I can hear the ship's bell, and that means she's close. It's hard to see her out the watchroom window."

Then we all heard a faint clang-clang above the rushing wind and crashing water.

Father hurried for his coat. "You're right. That's nearby." He glanced out the window. "The light is burning well. They see it, but if we hear their bell, they are in trouble. Get your coat, Richard."

They put on their coats and hurried into the dark storm. Mama told us to stay calm and went to one of the front windows. "Dear God," I heard her murmur prayerfully. A quarter of an hour passed. I struggled to hear, wanting to go to the window, but determined to obey Mama's directions to stay by the fire. Then a splintering crack echoed, louder than the wind and waves. Mama ran into the main room and snatched her coat from its peg. "Stay inside," she ordered, before running through the entryway and out the front door.

The boys and I flew to the front window. The revolving light above us cast alternating beams on the scene. A small vessel had wrecked on the rocks and wedged there precariously while the high waves regularly tossed saltwater over the it.

The boys and I held hands, fearfully watching and praying. Marian tugged at my skirts, but I refused to let her see.

Mama hurried in, and I ran after her into the kitchen. Her cold fingers fumbled with the matches as she struggled to light a candle. "Light this for me, please, Susan," she requested, trying to stop her chattering teeth. I took the wooden match, struck it, and the fire appeared. Touching it to the candle wick took only a second, and then I closed the protective lantern glass around the little light. Mama put her cold hands gently on either side of my face. "Susan, can you be brave? Run to the bedrooms. Get some of the quilts and wool blankets off the beds and carry them downstairs. Bring two or three to us outside."

"Yes, Mama," I replied, ready to help and with no time to think of being scared.

Ripping some blankets off the beds, I pushed them downstairs. "Do you want us to help?" Jacob asked, watching me struggle to lift three heavy blankets.

"No, I don't think Mama wants you outside. But you can get a few blankets and lay them over the chairs near the fire. Paul, mind Marian. Jacob, open the door for me."

The wind tried to keep me inside, away from the people who needed these blankets. I fought back, pushing forward, feeling the rain and cold biting through my dress. I struggled on, reaching the place where Mama stood with some men and two girls who had been rescued from the wreck. The newcomers huddled and looked terrified.

The water thundered on the rocks. The girls took the blankets with dazed looks but refused to follow Mama to the lighthouse. I stood there in the drenching rain, watching, terrified and proud all at the same time. Father pulled a man ashore while Uncle Richard half-assisted and half-carried another man. "That's everyone," one of the men standing near us shouted. Mama turned to the young ladies and led them toward the house.

Uncle Richard staggered near where I stood. The man he had been helping, fell on his knees, crying – but his sobs were muffled by the storm. He curled close to the earth. By the flashing light, I saw it was Inspector Milton.

"She's gone," he shrieked, his despair loud enough to be heard.

In an instant, Uncle Richard knelt in front of him, shaking his shoulders, trying to stop those frightful cries. "No," my uncle shouted back. "She's safe. Your daughter and the other girl were the first off the boat. I promise. She is safe."

Face to face, the two men stared at each other. The light flashed; I saw relief on Inspector Milton's face. The brief darkness in the lighthouse's flash pattern came. Then light again; I saw disbelief. Then, rage. "You!" he exploded. "It is you."

Chapter 22

In the house, the rescued folks crowded around the fire, trying to get warm. One young lady – probably the inspector's daughter, I thought – cried hysterically, and Mama tried to calm her. My teeth chattered, but I wasn't sure if it was just the cold or fear also. What would the inspector say and do? Would Father and Uncle Richard lose their jobs tonight? But they had also saved the inspector, his daughter, another lady, two other passengers, and the crew of the small vessel.

The lady, sitting near the fire with her back to the door, turned. Blue eyes, soaked blonde hair, and a drenched fashionable dress: Miss Elsie Shermann. She looked at me, but this time she didn't smile. What was she doing here? Come to see the disaster she had caused? I almost wished she'd been drowned. Then I felt bad for thinking that.

Behind me in the entry hall, the angry inspector confronted my uncle and father, talking loud enough for everyone to hear. "You both lied to me." Father said something quietly. "No, neither of you are going anywhere," Inspector Milton insisted. "That light will be fine for ten minutes while I decide what has been happening around here."

I stood dripping in the doorway, listening with confusion and growing angry. Could Inspector Milton have no grace? Didn't he realize they'd just saved his life? I looked at Miss Elsie, expecting to see a triumphant expression. Instead, tears ran down her face.

For once, Uncle Richard did not evade questions, replying resignedly, "Sir, I have not lied. I have not told the entire truth, perhaps. But every question you ever asked me, I answered honestly."

"I have made a mistake. I am sorry and would like to explain," Father added.

The inspector paced across the hall twice, pounding his fist into his palm. Wheeling suddenly, he shouted, "I will not have a man who supported the Confederacy serving in my lighthouse district!"

"Perhaps we should sit down and talk reasonably," Father suggested. "There are some things that need explaining. For all of us." The three men pushed past me, leaving me beside the door, wondering if I should enter the lighted room or hide in the safety of the shadowy upstairs.

In the main room, the confrontation halted the process of drying wet clothes. The wet witnesses seemed to freeze in place, waiting to see what was about to happen. Mama sank into a chair, holding Marian, while the boys gathered around her. Father and Uncle Richard stood near the fireplace, facing Inspector Milton, who had seated himself in a chair and waited like an impatient judge. I slid down against the wall, wrapping my arms around my knees.

"I'm waiting, Mr. Bates," the inspector announced.

Straightening, Uncle Richard replied, "I will start from the beginning. For those of you who don't know me, I'm Richard Nathaniel Bates. From age eleven, I worked on merchant ships – starting as a cabin boy and working to become first mate and later captain."

"Get on with it. Get on with it," the inspector muttered. Uncle Richard ignored him. The others listened, not interested, but evaluating the story.

"On December 30, 1860, the merchant ship I sailed on took a cargo into Charleston Harbor. Unfortunately, creditors took the ship to cover gambling debts the ship owner and master had incurred. Some of you may recall that South Carolina was not real anxious to do business in December 1860? The state had seceded, trying to form a separate nation. The city – indeed, the entire state – was in secession and war fever with militia units being formed, and everybody looking forward to independence or a war."

I glanced at Father. He listened, his arms folded across his chest. Mama had pressed a trembling hand to her lips. Uncle Richard went on, looking directly at Inspector Milton.

"I stayed quiet for a while, looking for a ship to get away. Then the harbor was closed. I tried to find a way to get North, but without much success with the amount of money I had available at the time."

"As you well know, the war began on April 12, 1861, with the firing on Fort Sumter in Charleston Harbor. Then, the Rebels tried to enlist me. But I was too loyal to the Union and resolved that I would not fight against the United States. I got a band of hot-blooded secessioners after me. In my desperation to get away and not fight for the Confederacy, I heard about the merchant ships that wanted to trade with Europe, bringing goods to the South. I signed on a blockade runner as my way of escape. I planned to get to Europe, leave the ship, and get back to a Union state."

"However, on the first voyage, I was first mate, and they kept too close an eye on me for escape. On the second voyage, we ran to the West Indies. I got fever and chills, and by the time we reached Europe, I was too weak from the illness to make a return voyage."

I started to understand my uncle's story and mysteries. Loyalty to his country and beliefs had forced him to take a drastic step. But who was M. Jamison? Listening carefully, I hoped that secret would be revealed.

"But you did come back during the war," the inspector insisted, scuffing his wet boots on the floor.

Uncle Richard ignored him and went on. "I spent two years in Europe. Then was forced to return on a blockade runner to get away from an influential and dangerous person. I was allowed to leave as captain of the blockade runner. There were some dispatches that had been placed on my ship – something about ending the war. I agreed to run them into Confederate territory with the understanding that I did not know the contents of the messages. And that, sir, is when you found me." For the first time since beginning his narrative, Uncle Richard looked away from Inspector Milton, staring toward the darkened windows. "The storm left me two options as I approached the Carolina coastline: run back to sea and be captured by the Union warship or attempt to run my ship inland, hoping for an inlet or a sandy beach. It was not the first time I had sailed the Carolina coast. But this time it was dark."

He paused. I knew what he was going to say, what was coming next in the account. I longed to run to my uncle, hug him, and whisper that it was alright. I couldn't – he would tell the story on his own, in his own way, and overcome his captive secrets.

Uncle Richard took a deep breath and went on, stopping at the end of each phrase. "There was no light from the lighthouse, no guiding beacon. The ship ran aground, but not far enough. The waves tumbled the ship, and only five of the crew – myself included – survived."

He lifted his head and looked at the inspector proudly. "Yes, I was a blockade runner. An unarmed merchant man. I refused to fight for the Confederacy. It seemed the only option open to an able-bodied man in my situation. My loyalty cost me a great deal – more than any of you can ever comprehend, I'm afraid. That is all I can say."

Silence. Mama brushed away a tear. Father had uncrossed his arms. I still wondered. The rescued men listened intently, trying to understand what prompted this telling. The inspector's daughter had been weeping since the first mention of the war while Inspector Milton sat motionless. Miss Elsie had kept all expression and emotion from her face; with the exception of her quick drawn breaths, she could've been a graveyard statue.

"Mr. Arnold, would you like to add anything?" Inspector Milton asked.

Father stepped forward. "Yes. A document went missing from my desk recently. I have reason to suspect the culprit is now in this room." He slowly looked at each rescued person. Miss Elsie couldn't look him in the eye. "That document was private. Some may argue it should never have been written. For those of you who don't know what it was: a record book detailing the lighthouse service of my assistant, Richard Bates. He did nothing that interfered with his official duties. The record in the official log book is honest. However, I had my suspicions about his past, and he refused to tell us what had happened. In the beginning, I wanted a record as protection for myself and my family in case Mr. Bates took a drastic measure against himself or another person. A few weeks ago I stopped writing in the book, feeling that Mr. Bates had settled into lighthouse keeping."

The inspector uncrossed his arms and leaned forward. "If you did not intend to show it to anyone and you did not tell your lighthouse inspector about any odd behavior, why did you keep the record, Mr. Arnold?"

"I was influenced by my experience and a mistake which I made during my lightkeeping along Lake Erie during the war," Father replied, glancing at Mama. "There, in autumn 1864, two men came to my lighthouse, saying they were from the Lighthouse Board. It didn't take long for me to figure out they were lying. Beyond the official log book record which stated their fraudulent visit, I didn't write down my thoughts, observations, and suspicions. Three months later, the county was looking for Confederate spies after an attempted murder of a local mayor who was outspoken in support of Union. Further, rumors came that spies had tried to bribe county officials – the lighthouse keeper included – into creating or turning a blind eye to tampering with shore navigation beacons to cause disaster along that stretch of the lake. No one offered me a bribe, but I wished I'd kept a more detailed, private record of all visitors who came to the lighthouse in the previous months. The Rebels were not caught, and in the end, everyone concluded it was only a local disturbance caused by Confederate sympathizers. I resolved that in the future if I suspected any sort of problem which maybe shouldn't be in the official record, but I believed something was wrong, I'd keep a private record for my own purposes."

"Perhaps a wise decision," Uncle Richard said. "But why here? Why me?"

"You wouldn't talk about your past and were clearly troubled," Father replied, turning to Uncle Richard. "I'm not sure what was so bad about your story that you couldn't tell me or Harriet. We would've kept your confidence."

"He couldn't tell you," Miss Shermann said, standing and speaking quietly, "because he still has not told the entire story."

Uncle Richard exploded. "Just a minute, woman! What right did you have to come here? To take something without permission and use it against me? Against my entire family."

"I did take the record book. That was the first day I was here."

"See I told you!" Paul piped up.

Miss Elsie frowned at Paul, then continued. "However, on the second day and all the rest of the days we were here, I tried to put it back because I had discovered something about the person I'd been sent to spy on. In the end, I had to take it with me. I told the person who had sent me that I didn't find anything to share, but my father had seen me trying to dispose of the notebook and asked about it in front of the person." She looked at Inspector Milton. "That person threatened to reveal a part of my past that I would rather forget. I couldn't get the book back." She dared Uncle Richard, "Shall I tell the rest of the story? The part you aren't telling?"

"Enough, Miss Shermann. Sit down. He has told all that is necessary," Inspector Milton commanded. "I'm sorry, Mr. Bates, Mr. Arnold. You both tried to do the right and honorable thing. This past war has influenced thoughts, loyalties, and decisions. I should make a confession too." The inspector stood, tapping his wet, muddy boot on the floorboard. He looked at his daughter who hid her face in her hands. "My son was killed during the war. I have bitterness against the

Confederates, and I'm afraid I have taken it out on you, Mr. Bates."

He glanced down and clenched his fists to regain control. "I have blamed you for two reasons. First, because I found out about my son's death the night we captured you. Second, because you escaped when I wanted to make you pay for the death. It was wrong. You had nothing to do with the casualty. Can you forgive me? I can't blame you for my son's death, and I owe you a debt of gratitude for saving my daughter's life tonight."

They shook hands, both struggling to keep their composure. In a cracking voice, Inspector Milton said, "And I am sorry about the woman. I was sorry then, and I am more sorry now."

What woman? I thought. Margaret? If so, what was the secret?

Chapter 23

"What did you think, Mama?" I whispered. We were in the kitchen, cleaning up from making coffee and food for our storm refugees.

Father came into the kitchen before Mama answered. "I've assigned rooms and bedding for everyone. The little ones are tucked in our bed for now," he said. "Inspector Milton is in the watchroom, and I think he would prefer to be alone for a few minutes."

Mama turned away from him and busily closed and straightened the curtains at the kitchen window. "I'm sorry," Father said, standing close behind her.

"I'm sorry too, Samuel," she finally said, wiping her eyes. "I know you never meant to hurt my brother. You wanted him to stay, after all. I'm sorry I took my anger out on you these last few days." Father hugged her, whispering something I couldn't hear.

I took the stack of dried plates to the pantry shelf. Uncle Richard came into the kitchen. "I should've told you," he said. "I should've been completely honest. Then none of this would've happened."

Father reached out to shake Uncle Richard's hand, but my uncle pulled him into a hug. Mama joined, and I couldn't resist either. We stood there hugging, smiling – Mama crying happy tears – and feeling free. At that moment, I didn't want to be anywhere else. I didn't even want to see Jane or Anna. My family was all that mattered right then.

"Still haven't told the rest of the story," Miss Elsie said softly, from the doorway. "What would they all think then, Mr. Bates?"

Uncle Richard pretended he hadn't heard her. "There is something else I have to explain." He took a deep breath.

"Perhaps you're tired," Mama suggested to the nosy young woman. "You might feel better tomorrow if you get some good rest." Mama's expression sternly suggested she wanted Miss Elsie to go away, and she retreated from the doorway to a chair beside the fire.

Father started to shoo me to bed. "Let her stay, please," Uncle Richard said, closing the door to prevent Miss Shermann from joining us or watching.

He leaned on the sturdy kitchen table where the small lantern shone brightly and opened a photograph case he'd been holding. It was the photograph I'd accidentally seen. The beautiful woman stared from her case with a serene and peaceful expression. Mama picked up the case and looked questioningly at Uncle Richard; Father looked over her shoulder.

Uncle Richard swallowed, took a deep breath, and said quietly. "I was married. My wife died in the shipwreck on the Carolina coast."

The truth at last, and a truth I had not suspected. Father and Mama glanced at each other.

"Margaret," Uncle Richard said quietly. "Margaret Jamison was her maiden name. She was a Southerner. Her family supported the Confederacy and had moved to Glasgow at the beginning of the war. Her father was a powerful agent for the Confederate government, but I did not know that when we were first acquainted."

"When and how did you meet the Jamison Family and… Margaret?" Mama asked, clearly puzzled.

"When the blockade runner left me behind because of the fever's effects. Recovered, I found work in a chandlery shop, and the owner and Mr. Jamison were working together. I now know they were outfitting blockade runners, but I didn't realize what was going on until long after I'd fallen in love with Margaret."

"Was she a spy?" Father questioned.

"She was not. She hated the war, and we both agreed to have nothing to do with the conflict and to get back to America as soon as it was over. We were married on May 20, 1864. After that, Mr. Jamison treated me like a son, but started expecting me to participate in his secretive meetings. I learned too much about veiled threats and underhanded dealings. Margaret and

I became desperate to get away before we were entrapped in something truly dangerous."

"So you tried to get back to the United States?" Mama said.

"Yes. A couple months later, we were on the ship, heading back to America. I was the captain. Margaret and I had dispatches, but we did not know the contents. That was the understanding. I agreed to go back to America, but I did not want any part in the schemes. We had plans to sail to Wilmington to deliver the messages and then travel to Union captured territory and from there board a ship to take us back to New England."

He swallowed hard and looked down at his hands, absently touching where his wedding band should have been. "I was the captain of the ship, but I could not save the vessel or my wife. Margaret drowned. Margaret is dead. And that is why I didn't want to talk about or explain my past." He broke down and tried to escape, but Mama embraced her brother and wouldn't let him run.

Wide-eyed, I reached for the photograph, abandoned on the table. "Margaret," I whispered. "My aunt." I couldn't blame my uncle for his secretive sadness, but I wished he'd told us sooner.

"I'm sorry, Richard," Father said, when Mama let her brother go. "I thought you were only upset about the ship on the lake. I didn't realize the extent and reason of your grief."

Uncle Richard gave a quick nod. "Well, now you know all of it. I don't have any more secrets. And whether I stay or get dismissed, at least I've been completely honest with you. Maybe you could even trust me."

"I know I could," Father answered. He waited a moment, then asked, "Who is Miss Shermann?"

"She is Margaret's cousin. She was – might still be – a double spy. I know that from Mr. Jamison who used her information and was also betrayed by her, though I didn't know her name which is why I didn't recognize her. I'm guessing the inspector sent her here to spy on me, but I think when she found out I was Margaret's husband, she tried to save me." He lowered his voice. "I don't trust her, but there's nothing she can use for legitimate accusation."

He opened the door. The main room was empty.

Chapter 24

The next morning the sun lit the storm-clearing sky, the water danced roughly, and the small wrecked vessel had been pulled off the rocks and battered into pieces. One might imagine the storm and the revelations of last night were just dreams, except for the open feelings and smiles exchanged between my family and our unanticipated guests. After breakfast, the crewmen went outside to smoke pipes or cigars, Marian settled on the floor with her little wooden toys, and the boys and I helped Mama wash and dry a mountain of dishes. Father, Uncle Richard, and Inspector Milton disappeared into the parlor.

A while later, they came into the main room, smiling, and Inspector Milton said to Mama, "You won't have to move, ma'am. Now that everything has been fully explained and understood, I think it's best that Arnold and Bates continue as the keepers at Herdman Point. Furthermore, I'll be sending an account to the Board of the rescue and commending their service."

"Thank you, Inspector," Mama replied. "That is good news. Good news, indeed."

Father and Uncle Richard grinned. "I think we have some chores to do, Head Lighthouse Keeper," Uncle Richard said teasingly.

"Since the storm has cleared," Inspector Milton declared, "I believe my daughter and I, Miss Shermann, and the others will walk to town. I was taking the girls to spend a month with an aunt, and we had decided to make a seagoing excursion of the short trip. We all know how that turned out," he said, rolling his eyes. "She'll be worried when we do not arrive today, and I would like to send a telegram to let her know we were delayed, but safe. I don't want to keep you from your duties, gentlemen." His eyes twinkled. "So I'll go find my daughter and the others." He went out and closed the door behind him.

"Yahoo! We get to stay," Jacob shouted while Paul jumped up and down. Marian clapped her hands.

Joy filled me. My mind told me this would be a time when I would usually think of my friends and old home, but I didn't. I was happy to be here, with my family, with my uncle. Mattie darted by, and I scooped her up and spun around, giggling. "This is home," I squealed. "This is home."

"Alright, alright, settle down," Mama instructed, but she couldn't stop smiling. "We have a few chores of our own."

Our tasks were interrupted when the inspector gathered everyone together, said good-bye, and prepared to start. His daughter glanced around and asked, "Where's Elsie?"

"She was outside," I answered. "I saw her when I went to get water."

"Ah, yes. She's delaying Mr. Bates from his tasks," Inspector Milton muttered good-naturedly, glancing out the window. "Miss Arnold, would you run and tell her that we are departing and Miss Milton is concerned?"

I nodded, went out, and skipped toward the pair. Uncle Richard and Miss Elsie stood facing each other at the top of the path to the dock. As I came up, Uncle Richard said, "I've told all my secrets. I have nothing to be ashamed of – other than keeping them so long. I'm not afraid of anything you'll say to anyone."

"I wish I could tell all my secrets," she admitted, "but that would take too long. I want you to know that as soon as I knew you were Margaret's husband, I tried to protect you. I loved my cousin. We spent every summer together as girls. She had written to me and mentioned you, but she didn't tell about your work in the shop. Of course, my aunt told me about her...death. I tried to protect you," she repeated.

"I realize that. But you were caught in your own web."

"You must think I'm a terrible person," Miss Elsie said, still ignoring my presence though Uncle Richard had glanced at me. "Fine. No more secrets." Her lip quivered. "I've said I was a nurse during the war. That was true. But I was also a spy. But worse than that – it was a game to me. I spied for both sides. Traded information for power and permission to get to my father's hospital and prison. Despise me. I know you will. But I made a choice to survive and to save my father."

"But you sacrificed your loyalty," he answered.

"We have different views. I was loyal to my father. Whatever it cost me."

"We will not likely agree on this," Uncle Richard said. "You can't pick and choose which areas of life you want to be loyal. It's like keeping a lighthouse. You can't polish the brass and neglect the lens. You can't polish the lens and forget to fill the oil reservoirs. If you will be a lightkeeper, one must do everything humanly possible to keep that light burning – even the little seemingly insignificant things. If you will be a person of character, one must live strong character qualities in every area of life – work, family, marriage, beliefs, and country."

"As you said, we have different views." Her tone and expression softened, and she said, "If our experiences had been different, perhaps we could've been friends, Mr. Bates." Then she raised her head with a queenly expression. "Goodbye." She walked passed me; I saw that proud expression slip, and there were tears in her eyes.

Uncle Richard stood by me, and we watched her walk away. "Are you sorry she doesn't like you?" I asked.

"I couldn't trust her," he said simply. "It's not likely we would've been friends." He reached for my hand, and we walked back together.

In the afternoon, I carried my poetry book down to the main room, trying to decide what to do with my scribblings. Mama sat at the empty table, idly leaning her cheek on her hand and watching the waves through the window. "Are you alright?" I asked, touching her arm.

She looked up at me, and I could see she had been crying. "Yes. I'm fine. I just wish Richard could've told us before. Did he think we wouldn't approve?"

"I think he didn't know how to tell us," I replied. "Mama, I have to tell you something. Maybe I should've told you a long time ago…" I paused, and she looked at me questioningly. "I saw the picture of Margaret before Uncle Richard showed it to us. And I saw a book of maps and read a letter belonging to Uncle Richard. The picture was sitting out, and I saw it by accident. But the letter was in an envelope, and I opened it. The maps were hidden under his bed."

"Oh, Susan," Mama said sorrowfully. "Did you say anything to your uncle? Why didn't you tell Father or me?"

"No, I didn't ask him. I didn't tell because I was afraid I would be telling a secret that wasn't mine."

"I hope you won't do that again, Susan. Keeping secrets creates a burden you don't need to carry." She wiped away the couple of tears on my face and hugged me.

"Mama, I want to tell you something else." I took a deep breath. "I was unhappy. I didn't like it here in the beginning. You tried to talk to me, but I didn't want you to think I was weak because I missed my friends."

"Why would I think that, dear?"

"Because you are so strong. You liked it here. You didn't miss anyone."

"That's not completely true, Susan. I often miss my sister and my mother very much. I knew you missed Jane and Anna. That's alright. It's normal to miss your friends."

"I tried not to think about it, but sometimes I think that made me feel worse. I started writing poetry."

"Yes, I know," Mama said, looking puzzled.

"But I was writing because I didn't want to think about things. I wanted to create imaginary worlds. I wanted to escape from my loneliness. It didn't work."

"It usually doesn't, daughter. It's better to be completely honest and face your struggles instead of hiding from them. I hope you know that I want to help you. Come talk to me about your challenges."

"Thank you, Mama."

She smiled and patted my hand. "May I read your poems?"

"I don't like them so much anymore. I'm going to burn them." It was an impulsive idea, but when I said it I thought it was a good idea.

Mama looked at me, puzzled. "Why?"

"Because I don't need imaginary worlds anymore."

"Oh, daughter – keep your imagination. Your love of writing."

"I will. I think I'd like to keep a journal instead. Write about real things happening in our lives. Would that be alright?"

"It's a lovely plan," she approved.

The storm had brought autumn's chill, and Father had built up the fire for the late afternoon. I tore out the pages created in silence and loneliness. I knelt beside the fire, tossing the papers in. The heat curled the edges, and I watched as the flames ate the weeks of escape. Fiery light from ruins, burning to give way to better thoughts. Mattie curled beside me as I opened my notebook and ran my hand over a clean page.

Someday soon, I'd write a letter to Anna and Jane, telling them about the shipwreck, my finished sampler which now hung in the parlor, and the molasses cookies Mama had promised to teach me to make next week. Today, I'd start my journal. Carefully, I wrote my name: Susan Rose Arnold. The year: 1867. Herdman Point Lighthouse.

Uncle Richard came into the room, laughing at something Jacob said. He gathered the boys at the table, saying, "Want to look at my sea charts?" He opened the book. "This is a map of Scotland."

"What's this one?" Paul asked.

"Wilmington Harbor. That's in North Carolina. See, if you're ever going to sail there you have to…" He leaned over the map, lowering his voice to tell the boys an adventurous tale.

Father entered, carrying Marian who'd just woken from her nap. She started trying to talk in her baby way when she saw Mama sitting on the rug, waiting to play blocks with her.

"Sun's close to the horizon," Father announced as he set Marian down. "I'll prepare the light. You're fine," he said to Uncle Richard as he started to leave the table. "Boys, in a few minutes, bring in the flag." They looked up from the maps and nodded.

"May I come with you, Father?" I asked. When he agreed, I took my blank notebook and hurried after him, Mattie racing at my heels. We climbed the stairs to the upper story, then higher to the watchroom.

"Watch your step," Father instructed as we went up the ladder to the lantern.

The lens sparkled in the light from the setting sun. "Beautiful, isn't it?" he questioned, examining the light-giving equipment. I watched Father's steady hands checking and preparing the lamps and cleaning invisible specks of dust from the lens with a cotton cloth.

"Can I go out on the walk?"

"For a couple minutes. It's not too windy, but hold onto the railing." He opened the small door for me to scramble through. "Be careful not to drop your notebook."

The crisp sea air swirled in a gentle breeze, tugging at my skirt and loose strands of hair. I squinted into the sunlight. Soon the sun would drop behind the hills, and the sea would grow dark. Then – as though mirroring the example of the sun – our light would come to life and witness into the gloom. A warning to the wandering. A guide to those at sea. A light in the darkness.

Loyalty, I thought. Once I had wondered what it meant, but now I knew. It was my father's courage. My mother's devotion to home and family. Loyalty was my family and our lighthouse.

The American flag fluttered in the breeze, a symbol of national allegiance and lighthouse duty. Once I'd wondered about the war. I still had questions, and I might never fully understand it all. I thought about everyone I knew whose lives were affected by it. Some had chosen to tell their secrets from the war. Others would live with dark memories from the conflict for the rest of their lives. Shadows of the past surround all of us, I decided. My past memories and loneliness had been my secret. Uncle Richard, Father, Inspector Milton, and Miss Shermann's experiences had clouded their perceptions and choices.

I opened the cover of my notebook. Under the lighthouse name, I wrote Father's words, "Trust has to be earned. Loyalty can't be bought. Where there is hard work, loyalty, and family love, there is light."

The real shadows lengthened around me, deepening the ocean's blue and the sky's gray. Behind me, the lamps within the lens came to life, and the burning light reflected and reached out to chase away the shadows. Like character and choices illuminating our pasts and guiding our futures. The wind teased the empty pages, daring me to fill them with the present, not the past.

I took a deep breath and gripped my pencil. But the words would not come – I was too happy to write.

Author's
Historical Notes

Herdman Point Lighthouse, the Arnold Family, Richard Bates, Inspector Milton, the Shermanns, and other characters in the story are fictional. Herdman Point Lighthouse does not exist, and you won't find these characters in historical archives. However, months of research – some of it at a lighthouse location – were the foundation for this story, and the author has done her best to ensure accuracy in the historical "snapshots," situations, and aspects of this story.

Fictional Herdman Point Lighthouse is based on templates and floorplans of real lighthouses along the Long Island Sound and in the New England region. Aspects of the coastline and weather also reflect reality, and lists of wildlife and native plants were studied to incorporate some seaside flavor.

Lighthouses have been an important – often forgotten part – of American History. The first known lighthouse built in the country was constructed in 1716 on an island near the entrance of Boston Harbor, and others were also built before the War For Independence. During George Washington's presidency, Congress passed a resolution moving all lighthouses from state and local control to the control of a federal agency (August 7, 1789). In the early 19th Century, many lighthouses were built along the coastlines, but lightkeeping standards were not uniform or well enforced. After complaints of mismanagement, investigations occurred, and Congress established the U.S. Lighthouse Board in 1852 to oversee the construction and administration of the lighthouses. Inspectors routinely visited every lighthouse in their district to ensure that the rules and regulations prescribed by the Board were followed.

The Bureau of Lighthouses (U.S. Lighthouse Service) was created in 1910 and oversaw the American lighthouses until 1939 when the Coast Guard took over the administration. Today, the Coast Guard continues to look after the automated aids to navigation, but many historic lighthouses have been decommissioned. Happily, lighthouses have faithful friends, and many have been protected and preserved by national parks, state parks, historical societies, or special groups for lighthouse preservation.

Looking for real stories about American lighthouse keepers? There are wonderful accounts; find a lighthouse non-fiction history book, search for websites, or visit Sarah's author website to start. The keeper's family was allowed to live at the lighthouse if the location permitted (there were some locations that were too dangerous for families). As highlighted in the story, keepers, assistants, and their families were required to follow the rules, and most did.

The American Civil War (1861-1865) presented challenges to the American shoreline and maritime community. Eleven Southern states decided they wanted to form a separate nation and seceded; President Lincoln and the Northern states determined to keep the Union together. The four year war resulted in a reunited country and thousands of casualties. Union ships patrolled the Southern coast, blockading and trying to prevent import/exports, messages, or diplomats from leaving the Confederacy. In an effort to hinder the Union ships, the Confederates darkened and frequently destroyed lighthouse lenses and oftentimes the structures. During the Reconstruction Era (1865-1877), many lighthouses along the Southern coast were rebuilt.

Blockade runners took cotton and information out of the Confederacy. Many slipped to the West Indies and exchanged cargo or waited for favorable conditions to cross the Atlantic to France, England, Scotland, Ireland, or other European countries. Returning to the Confederacy, these unarmed steam-powered merchant ships carried messages, luxury items, weapons, and valuable medical supplies. If a blockade runner could not reach a Southern port and was going to be captured, a captain might decide to run his ship aground or into a narrow inlet; sometimes, this worked and the vessel would be beached. Other times, like in the story, the results were disastrous. Many blockade runner steam ships were constructed and outfitted in the British Isles, creating a dangerous game of business, politics, and war. Confederate agents roamed European countries, involved in discussions, plots, and deals while leaving limited information – or nothing – for historians to discover.

For more historical details, please visit:
www.Gazette665.com

Acknowledgements

Working on this third book for publication presented challenges. After the publication of my first historical novel (*Blue, Gray & Crimson*), I thought I would simply do my research, settle down, and write the second book. *Lighthouse Loyalty* – originally supposed to be that second book – took an honorable third debut in Gazette665's publishing plan. Far from my rosy ideals of writing a second novel, this book struggled through writing and editing… and nearly landed in the garbage can on two occasions. I have decided to mention that drama for two reasons: first, to encourage other writers working on a second book (keep writing), and second, to set the stage and say "thanks" to the few people who knew the struggles and told me – in various ways, tones, and expressions – to stay true to the history and my own ideas for story-craft.

A sincere "Thank You" to my loyal editing and proofreading team: Susan Bierle, Beth Esposito, Robert Rasband, Shawn Bierle, and Nathan Bierle. You helped me finesse this story and encouraged me to think deeply and be brave enough to write it.

Robert and Nancy Munson – It's sometimes hard to know where to begin expressing appreciation to the creators of an original idea. I had no idea how long this research and writing journey would last when I agreed to meet with you at Old Point Loma Lighthouse to talk about story possibilities and explore the lighthouse. I appreciated your research guidance, ideas, and candor through the writing process, and your willingness to let the story become mine, one with secrets and struggles. Hopefully, this book meets your expectations, reaching and inspiring many. "Write a book about lighthouses." Thank you for the suggestion and support.

Mark and Cheryl Schoenberger – Mark, thank you for the reams of email correspondence about maritime history during the early stages of research on this project and for sharing your stories about sailing with this land-lubber author. Cheryl, the original cover artwork is amazing; thank you for working with my ideas and insisting that they conform to the rules to make a true work of art.

Old Point Loma Lighthouse – is it strange to thank a location or inanimate object? Probably. Still it wouldn't be right to end this section without mentioning the historic lighthouse that I explored and revisited many times. Perhaps some of the best ideas came while sitting in the watchroom. And I'm grateful for the inspiration.

About the Author

S arah Kay Bierle, a historian, writer, and living history enthusiast, has been interested in American history for many years. Her fascination with maritime history began in her early teens when she read about early explorers and early naval history but wasn't really developed until challenged to write a book about lightkeeping in nineteenth century America. Sarah enjoyed researching and discovering the Civil War's impact on American maritime and individual lives.

Sarah was homeschooled K-12, completed an accelerated distance learning program for college, graduated from Thomas Edison State University with a BA in History, and currently serves as co-managing editor for Emerging Civil War. Sarah believes in dedicated research, reading good literature, and participating in hands-on historical learning. Her love of knowledge and teaching has involved her in living history, blogging, and volunteering at Cabrillo National Monument's lighthouse, allowing her to share her belief that "history is about real people, real actions, and real effects, and it should inspire us today."

When not researching or writing, Sarah enjoys spending time with her parents and siblings, baking, playing music, quilting, or visiting with close friends. She desires to share a message of hope through her daily life and her writing.

To order books,
find historical resources,
or contact the author,
please visit:

www.Gazette665.com

www.ingramcontent.com/pod-product-compliance
Lightning Source LLC
Chambersburg PA
CBHW072050170626
46813CB00004B/1280